Death Rites

Wendy Cartmell

Costa Press

Copyright © Wendy Cartmell 2016
Published by Costa Press

ISBN: 9781521329825
Imprint: Independently published

Wendy Cartmell has asserted her right under the Copyright Designs and Patents Act 1998 to be identified as the author of this work.
All characters and events in this publication, other than those in the public domain, are fictitious and any resemblance to real persons, living or dead is purely coincidental
This is a work of fiction and not meant to represent faithfully military, or police, policies and procedures. All and any mistakes in this regard are my own.
Inspired by a friend and fellow writer.

Praise for Wendy Cartmell
'A pretty extraordinary talent' –
Best Selling Crime Thrillers
'This is genre fiction at its best, suspense that rivets and a mystery that keeps you guessing.' –
A R Symmonds on Goodreads.

Also by Wendy Cartmell

Sgt Major Crane books:

Steps to Heaven
40 Days 40 Nights
Honour Bound
Cordon of Lies
Regenerate
Hijack
Glass Cutter
Solid Proof

Crane and Anderson books:

Death Rites
Death Elements
Death Call

Emma Harrison Mysteries

Past Judgement
Mortal Judgement
Joint Judgement

One

Six months earlier....

It was stifling inside the black hood and he was sure the pointed top was wilting in the heat; just as he was. The smell of the blood in the chalice was making him feel sick and, if he was honest, the last thing he wanted to do was to drink it. But the humiliation of not joining in the ceremony was probably worse than taking a drink. Just.

He and his fellow supplicants formed a semi-circle around an altar, upon which lay a young child: she was very much alive but drugged to keep her quiet while the bloodletting took place. Her long blond hair was in dramatic contrast to the plain black shift that she wore. Her face was white, lips flesh coloured and only the faintest rising and falling of her chest indicated that she was breathing. On the back of one hand was a needle that fitted snugly into her vein. Attached to the needle was a small plastic tube that allowed her precious blood to drip out into the chalice. She could have been asleep, instead of unconscious. Around her were placed seven candles, six black and one white, their flames guttering and smoking in the hot fetid air.

Normally children were banned from attending these rituals, the only exception being the Satanic baptism, which was specifically designed to involve infants, and such a baptism was taking place in the basement of a remote house in the dead of night. It was a ceremony deemed to be necessary to override any Christian or other religious ceremonies that the child may have been subjected to before joining the Satanic Church. He wasn't so sure it was necessary himself, but then all the churches had their rules, didn't they? He guessed it was no different to a Catholic first communion or a Jewish Bar Mitzvah and so he'd decided he may as well play along. Let's face it he had nothing better to do that night. And as he was moving soon, he'd thought he'd better make the most of the last meeting he would be attending.

As the chalice was passed to him he muttered the rite: Cursed are the lambs of God for they shall be bled whiter than snow.

Taking the tiniest of sips but still gagging on the foul taste of the blood, he just about managed to swallow it instead of coughing it out and spraying it all over the child. Thankful that he'd managed to get through it, he passed the cup to the next in line. To be fair, the group had tried to adhere as closely to the ritual as they could, using the rules described in the Satanic rituals, or dramatic performances as they were sometimes called. They followed the suggestions of the clothing to be worn, the music to be used and actions to be taken. It was said that the pageantry and theatricality was intended to engage the participant's senses on all levels. He could relate to that, for apart from the blood, the rest of it was definitely working for him.

All the males wore black robes and hoods but the young women were encouraged to make themselves attractive to the males present. As a result he was surrounded by a surfeit of black leather and rubber, long shiny thigh length boots and even the odd whip or two. Everyone wore the sign of sulphur around their necks. The intent of the women to stimulate sexual feelings amongst the men was exciting and he couldn't wait for the bloody ceremony to be over, so they could get on with the really interesting part, the part that started once the ceremony ended.

The Church of Satan smashed all concepts of what a 'church' was supposed to be. It was a temple of indulgence, where one could openly defy the temples of abstinence that had previously been built. Rather than an unforgiving, unwelcoming place, as so many of the church's built by religions that worshiped God were, theirs was a place where you could go to have fun. It was a religion based on self-indulgence, of carnality (of the here and now instead of the there and then), and, most importantly to him, of pleasure instead of self-denial

At last the final person drunk from the chalice, the welcome sound of the bell ringing nine times rang around the room, signalling the end of the ceremony. The formal part over, it was time for the only reason he was there. It was time for the fun to start….

Two

Today…

"When you wish upon a star, makes no difference who you are," Bethany sang in her head. She would have sung out loud, but her throat was raw and sore from crying. Oh and screaming. There had been a lot of screaming. She remembered that at least. The rest of it she just wanted to blank out and singing that song helped her do just that.

Shivering, whether from cold or fear she wasn't quite sure, she pulled the thin blanket over her shoulders and tried to tuck it around her body, so no cold air could get in. She wriggled down into her cocoon and imagined she was a butterfly, ready to burst from the confines of her sheath that kept her safe from predators, until she was ready, formed and changed into a beautiful creature. The land-bound caterpillar shrivelled, lying decaying on the forest floor.

Would she be safe, lying on a filthy mattress, covered by a smelly blanket? She knew she wouldn't. But no one had been to see her in a while. She felt she was safe for now. But then, in horror, she wondered if they'd forgotten about her? Moved on to another young girl? That thought was worse. If that were the case, she'd never get out of there. She'd stay in the filthy cell until she died from starvation, or dehydration, or whatever it was that you died from.

She'd been snatched from the park. Or at least that was the last place she remembered being in. Vague memories of ice cream, that tinkling music and chocolate sauce. She thought she'd fallen asleep after eating the ice cream and woken up here. Wherever here was.

She'd no idea how long ago that had been. She'd wanted to scratch the days on the wall, like she'd seen in the films. But she had nothing to scratch with and anyway the light never went off. The dirty bulb high in the ceiling provided a weak yellow light all the time, so she soon became disoriented, having no way to discern day from night, or night from day. She was fed at irregular intervals, a plate with a shop bought sandwich, a piece of fruit and a bottle of water. She'd thought she could count every time she was fed, thinking that would help tell her how long she'd been there. She was constantly hungry, so thought they only fed her once a day and so it should have been easy to count the meals. But as her strength waned, she became confused and after five, or was it six meals, she couldn't remember what the last number had been.

She closed her eyes, determined to try and get some sleep, pulling the blanket over her head to shut out some of the light, when she heard footsteps. She thought they sounded like her dad's boots. Her eyes flew open and she held her breath and listened. Hard. But there was no other sound. It seemed it wasn't time for another visit, or for another meal. She was safe for now. But her limbs wouldn't obey her mind. They began to shake again and she wondered if she was becoming addicted to whatever it was they gave her to keep her sleepy. Not so much willing and able, but oblivious. She fancied it was something they put in the water, but not in every bottle. Sometimes she felt fine after drinking it. At other times she would rapidly fall asleep and upon awakening had no recollection of what, if anything, had taken place. Just that the backs of her hands were sore and bruised. She felt like one of her Barbie dolls, to be played with for a while and then thrown back into the toy box. Discarded. Until the next time.

Tears tracked small rivulets through the dirt on her face, their salty taste coating her lips. Angrily she dashed them away and sniffed back the others threatening to fall from her eyes. She wouldn't break. She wouldn't give in. She wouldn't stop hoping. Hoping that one day this would be over and she'd be back home in Birmingham with her family.

The shuffling had started again. She was sure it was boots. It couldn't be mice or rats; they would scratch along the floor with their claws. Someone was making their way towards her cell in this cold basement that was her home now. She fancied it was a basement at any rate. The dirt floor, the wooden steps that she could see from the small square opening in the door of her prison climbing up the far wall. The damp, fetid air, the lack of windows, yes, she was sure it was a basement.

Scrabbling up the mattress, she curled into the corner, covering herself with the blanket from head to toe. Clamping her hands over her ears she began again to sing the song in her head. "Anything your heart desires will come to you."

The blanket was grabbed and thrown off her. She kept her eyes shut and her hands over her ears, shrinking even further into the corner. What did he want? Why hadn't she been drugged? Perhaps she hadn't drunk enough of the water? But it was too late now. Perhaps if she pretended to be unconscious he'd leave her alone. She was good at pretending. As a hand was placed on her arm, a large hand, a man's hand, she couldn't pretend anymore. She screamed a scream that burst out of her, despite her sore throat. She kept screaming, batting the hand off her arm, struggling as two hands grabbed her arms, kicking with her bare feet at the solid bulk of the man who was trying to hurt her and screaming, still screaming, until she was crushed against a body and rocked, rocked like a baby, rocked until she stopped struggling.

A hand caressed her hair, stroking her head over and over, and his voice whispered, "It's alright. You're safe now. I'm a policeman. I've come to take you home. Your wish has been granted."

He rose from the floor, his strong arms lifting her as though she were no more than a paper doll. "I'm going to cover your head with the blanket," he said. "Just to protect your eyes. Okay?"

She managed a small nod against his shoulder, still unsure that it was really happening: that she was being rescued. Her nightmare was finally over. With her head safely covered, she felt him walk up the wooden stairs, her body bumping against his as he climbed each tread, going up the stairs she'd fantasised clambering up for so long.

Once up the stairs, he moved quickly through what she imagined to be the house belonging to the basement and burst out of the front door, her head still covered by the blanket, through which daylight weakly filtered.

"I'm taking you to an ambulance," he said, his voice

rumbling in his chest and she managed another small nod. Bethany heard the creaking of the springs as they entered the vehicle and he placed her gently onto a hard bed, so she was sitting on it with her toes touching the floor. "There's someone here waiting for you," he continued. "So I'm going to take the blanket off your head."

The lights in the ambulance were stronger than she'd imagined. Even though she thought she'd prepared herself for the glare, she had no choice but to squint and hold up her hand against the lights. Through scrunched up lids she saw her mother sitting opposite, arms open, face wet with tears. Without any conscious thought, Bethany tipped forward to fall into her arms.

But instead of landing against the soft bosom of her mother, she fell face first onto the flea ridden, ripped mattress in her basement cell.

Three

The living nightmare seemed without end. Sgt Major Tom Crane couldn't stop re-experiencing the accident every time he closed his eyes. Each dawn he awoke drenched in sweat from the dreams he couldn't run away from, no matter how hard he tried. Once fully awake, the pain kicked in, yet another reminder that the accident had really happened. He was trapped in a broken body. Everything he held dear had been ripped from him. His job, his house, his way of life, his career and his mates. Gone. All gone in an instant.

Shivering in his damp tee-shirt, Crane struggled to sit and then once upright swung his good leg out of the bed, grabbing the gammy one and dragging it over to meet the other. As expected, the first few steps were agony as he stumbled his way to the bathroom. It was as if a gremlin had a dagger and was twisting the point round and round in his hip joint. Actually not one, but what felt like a whole family of the little buggers. He hated those gremlins with a passion. They would pop up at the most unexpected of times, poking and prodding with their knives, making his leg buckle; an attack that more often than not ended with him tumbling to the floor.

Crane turned on the shower and as he waited for the hot water to run through, he peeled off his tee-shirt and boxer shorts. The scars on his leg were beginning to fade, but the mental ones, he knew, would take much longer. As he stepped into the shower, luxuriating in the hot jets of water, try as he might, he couldn't shake the memories.

A split second was all it had taken for the stupid soldier driving the lorry to make the decision to drive off, before Crane was safely in the back of it. The vehicle had jerked forward, bowling Crane against the back board that should have stopped him from falling out. But the two soldiers tasked with securing the board hadn't had time to complete the action before the lorry kangarooed off and so Crane felt himself falling backwards out of the lorry. As his body hit the floor, everything went mercifully black.

He was later told that the official enquiry into the accident had proven that the soldier driving the lorry was to blame. The driver thought he'd heard the double tap that indicated he could safely move off. But it turned out the taps he had heard were for the lorry next to him. The only good thing about the accident was that Crane had been in a lorry parked outside Provost Barracks on Aldershot Garrison, instead of on exercise in the middle of the Brecon Beacons, meaning that an ambulance arrived quickly, rushing him to Frimley Park Hospital.

When he'd regained consciousness Crane had been horrified to find himself in hospital with his left leg elevated and some sort of metal contraption wrapped around it. Machines blinked at him, tubes went in and out of his body and he was in the grip of excruciating pain that started in his left hip and shot all the way down his leg to his toes. Panic had gripped him and he'd started screaming.

That was pretty much where the dream ended and the corporeal suffering began. Crane was now out of hospital, but heavily reliant on pain killers and a stick. He refused to sit in a wheelchair and was determined to work his way through the pain and treatment. From the start he was convinced he could fully recover and return to work. The problem was that the British Army hadn't agreed with him. They'd described his determination to return to full health as valiant, but pointed out that the surgeons and doctors in charge of his care had a very different prognosis. They said his shattered hip would mend, but because of it being kept immobile after surgery so his broken femur, tibia and fibula could heal, it would mean constant pain from the hip replacement and restricted movement, more so than if he'd had a normal recovery. Crane was unwilling to accept that diagnosis, but it hadn't mattered. The Army had spoken and just like that his career was over.

He wouldn't have minded so much if he'd been injured in a war zone whilst doing something worthwhile. Helping rebuild a war torn country and instructing new recruits in the local military police, something he'd done with some success a few years ago. Maybe if his leg had been shattered by an IED, or bullets even, he could have handled it better. But to be medically retired because he fell out of the back of a bloody lorry, well that was embarrassing in the extreme. Who would have thought the great Sgt Major Crane could be laid so low by an inexperienced soldier?

Left by himself for most of the day, as his wife Tina had returned to work in a local bank, he battled his demons on his own. Sometimes he was mentally strong enough to go through the exercises the physiotherapist had insisted he do every day. But on other days he felt suffocated by a cloak of hopelessness and lay in bed, helpless, bitter, angry and unwilling to interact with anyone.

Towelling himself dry, and then rubbing his short dark curly hair, Crane was glad that Tina and Daniel were in the house, it being Saturday. If he had been on his own he realised it would have been a rabbit hole kind of day. Once the gremlins forced his mind down into the warren of depression, he wouldn't have been able to find his way out. Limping back into the bedroom to dress, he realised the role that Tina was playing in his recovery was pivotal. She was stoically accepting of the situation and did her best to cheer him up, using their son Daniel as a beacon of hope; trying to shine a light into the blackness of his all-consuming depression. She refused to be brow beaten by his illness and carried on serenely, as if he were the old Tom, not the new bleak monster he sometimes changed into. Taking her lead, he did his best to try to ignore the melancholy, but it didn't always work and on those days he would stamp angrily around the house, railing against life, the army, fate, God and anyone else he could think of.

Determined not to be that man, at least not today, Crane hobbled down the stairs to join his family.

Four

After the dream that had seemed so real, Bethany resolved to take any chance she could to escape. She could feel herself getting weaker and weaker. She had to be strong. But strong in her head, as she was no match for the large man who came to bring her food and drink. She wasn't stupid. She knew she had no fighting skills, she had no weapons. All she had was a burning desire to get out of her prison and back home to her family.

She wondered again - where was she? Was she still in Birmingham? Had anyone noticed she'd gone missing? There were still no clues as to her location. If she ever left the room it was when she was drugged and so had no memory of it. Very few sounds filtered down to where she was. Despite concentrating on listening as hard as she could, she only got the faintest rustle of the leaves in the wind or the drip, drip, drip of the rain. Today there was neither and so she heard the footsteps clearly.

Backing into the corner of the room, making herself as small as possible, she watched the door. As the footsteps became louder, her heartbeat raced. The sound whooshed in her ears, rather like Mum's washing machine when it was rinsing the clothes. It was the thought of her mum that did it. She began to cry, her tears plopping on the mattress like the rain she occasionally heard outside.

The door creaked open and there he was, filling the door with his bulk. To Bethany he seemed huge; a bear of a man, or a gorilla. Either way he frightened her.

"You alright?"

He'd never spoken before, so the sound of his deep, grumbling voice made her gasp and cry even harder.

"You hurt?"

She managed to shake her head in reply.

"Brought some food."

He placed a tray on the floor and she saw through her tears the usual sandwich and bottle of water.

"I want to go home," she whispered.

"What? I can't hear you," and he moved closer.

She said it again, but the lump in her throat made the words stick there as well.

"What?"

He took another two steps forward, so he was now within touching distance. That frightened Bethany even more, but she screwed up her courage and screamed in his face, "I want to go home!" pouring into those few words all the anger she felt towards this man who she didn't know and who didn't know her.

The large man jumped back in surprise.

"Get out," she screamed. "Get out and leave me alone!" terrified that he was going to take her somewhere and do whatever it was he did when she was there. The injuries on the backs of her hands throbbed in time with her racing heart.

He turned and bolted for the door, slamming it behind him and she could hear his boots thumping up the wooden steps. Relieved that he'd gone, she gradually calmed down and looked down at the tray on the floor. She was desperate for water, but too afraid to drink it in case it made her fall asleep again. But she thought it might be alright to eat the sandwich.

Easing herself off the mattress, she put her bare feet on the floor. As she sat there, trying to decide if it was okay to eat, she felt a rush of cold air playing on her feet and legs. It must be windy outside. But she'd never felt a draught before. Standing up, she hobbled over to the door, to see if she could hear anything from the other side. As she put her ear to the wood it moved slightly. Putting her fingers on the door, she tentatively pushed on it and it opened slightly. Jumping back in surprise, she realised that maybe, just maybe, the man had forgotten to lock it when he left. This could be her chance…

Five

"Got a strange one here for you, guv."

DI Anderson sighed. What was it with this place? Aldershot was supposed to be a quiet backwater in the south of England, not a magnet for strange cases. And why did he always get the strange ones, especially on a Monday morning? He suspected it was because others flatly refused to take them, citing all sorts of excuses for their reluctance to help; whereas Anderson knew he was a sucker for a difficult case and, more importantly, so did his colleagues. And so he leaned back in his chair, tried and failed to tame his thinning grey hair that was standing on end again, and took off his reading glasses. Often he forgot and left them on, ending up peering myopically at his colleagues.

"Go on, then," he sighed, throwing his glasses on the desk in his office in the CID room at Aldershot Police Station. "Hit me with it."

"A child was found wandering early this morning, nearly naked and covered in strange markings."

"Eh?" Anderson sat up straight in his chair in his cubby hole of an office. "You serious?"

"Unfortunately I am, sir."

"What sort of strange markings?"

The young police officer consulted his notes. "Not sure, sir, that's all the information I have."

"Name?" Anderson barked.

"DC Douglas, sir."

"No, what's the child's name you idiot!"

"Oh, sorry," the young man flushed, his round, red face reminding Anderson of a beetroot. "No one has any idea, sorry."

"For God's sake, Douglas, stop saying sorry. And stop playing with your tie. Not that it matches your shirt. Is purple 'in' these days?"

"Yes, sir, I mean..."

"Age?"

"The doctors think she's about 11 years old."

"Where is she?"

"Frimley Park Hospital, sir. A uniformed PC is sitting with her."

"Right," Anderson said, forgetting about Douglas' purple tie and pink shirt. "Check missing persons, check with the Garrison that a child hasn't been reported missing to them, get a family liaison officer out of uniform and over to the hospital to relieve the uniformed PC, get a copy of the statement of the member of the public who found her and start searching CCTV in the vicinity of where she was found. Have forensics been called?"

"No idea, sir."

"Then find out and if no one has been called out then send someone to the hospital ASAP. Right then," Anderson grabbed his tweed jacket off the back of his chair, "I'm off."

"Where to, sir?"

Anderson gave the young man a withering look and

felt such a stupid question didn't warrant an answer. His hand went to his mobile to call Crane and see if he wanted to tag along, but then he remembered that Crane was out of the army and out of action. He must stop doing that, he berated himself, but old habits die hard.

***

Upon reaching Frimley Park Hospital, he got directions to the ward where the child was recovering from her as yet unknown ordeal and walked through the myriad of corridors, all of which seemed to smell of antiseptic and cabbage. He finally reached the correct ward and was shown to the child's room by a nurse.

"We felt it best that she be in a room on her own. Much quieter for her," the nurse said as they walked down the ward.

"How is she?"

"I'll call the doctor who will come up and see you."

"Is she talking?"

"As I said, the doctor will be up shortly."

Anderson gave up questioning her as she clearly wasn't going to offer an opinion. Stopping outside the room, he nodded his thanks to the officious nurse and paused before going in. Looking through the glass panel in the door, he saw a young girl lying motionless on a bed that seemed to swamp her. Her eyes were closed, her arms by her side lying on top of the blanket that was covering her. Along both arms crudely drawn swirls and symbols could be seen. They looked as if they had been painted on by a particularly bad artist. A bag of clear fluid was dripping something into the back of her hand, but that seemed to be the only treatment she was receiving. There were no beeping monitors, so Anderson surmised she must be in a stable condition. Her skin was almost translucent, dark bruises brushed her eyes and to be honest she looked as though she were dead. He wondered what the hell she had been through and that thought sent a shudder through him.

"Guv?" a soft voice asked.

"What?" Anderson turned to see a woman standing next to him.

"Sorry to startle you," she replied. "PC Victoria Fleming, FLO, out of uniform as requested."

"Oh, right, I was just looking…" Anderson gestured to the window.

"Poor kid," the PC said as she joined Anderson. "And we've no idea what happened to her?"

"No," Anderson took a breath and turned to face the FLO. "I want you to sit with her, so someone is there when she wakes up. Take the place of the uniformed officer. I just thought that a uniform might scare her. I'll update you as soon as the bloody doctor turns up."

"Right, guv," Fleming said and grabbed a bag from the floor.

"Fleming?"

"Yes, guv?"

"What the hell is in that bag? Don't tell me it's your lunch?"

Fleming smiled. "Well, not just my lunch. I grabbed 2 or 3 children's books as I left the station. I thought that reading to her, once she wakes up, would be a good way of engaging with her."

Anderson nodded his appreciation and Fleming slipped in the room to relieve the uniformed officer.

Six

While waiting for the doctor, Anderson called DC Douglas. "Got anything for me yet?" he barked without any preamble, realising as he did so that it seemed he'd picked up some bad habits from Crane over the years.

"Um, no, guv. Should I?"

Anderson could hear the tremble in the lad's voice and decided to be a bit kinder to him.

"Okay, let's go through my requests. Is someone checking missing persons?"

"Yes, guv, DS Bullock is."

"Good. What about that witness statement?"

"Got it and I've asked the Farnborough CCTV centre to scan the relevant areas," said Douglas, his voice growing in confidence.

"And forensics?"

"A CSI is on his way to you now."

"Good work, Douglas. What about the Garrison?"

"I've spoken to Sgt Williams and he promised to get back to me on that one."

"Right. I'll be back in the station once the forensic evidence has been collected…"

"And you are?" The obnoxious tone riled Anderson,

who hadn't heard anyone approach him.

He closed his phone, cutting off DC Douglas and turned to see a young man, of about Douglas' age, who was surely too young to be a doctor, dressed in green scrubs with a lanyard around his neck sporting a plastic ID card. "DI Anderson," he replied. "Aldershot Police."

"Oh, right, Dr Hammond," the young man extended his hand in what seemed to be a gesture of apology. "Sorry about that, but we can't be too careful."

Anderson shook the proffered limb, which was clammy, and Anderson wondered why. Perhaps it was nothing more than the strange circumstances of the arrival of his patient. "What can you tell me about her?"

Consulting a file he held in his other hand, the doctor said, "When she arrived she was unconscious. Her clothes consisted of nothing more than a black shift dress and it was torn and dirty."

"Where's the dress," Anderson interrupted.

"In a bag, in her locker, in the room. As I was saying, her feet were bare and as a result they are red and sore, with cuts all over the soles of her feet. As you can see, her arms are covered with those strange symbols."

"Has she been washed?"

"What? No I don't think so."

"Has a forensic expert been called?"

"No idea, DI Anderson. I would have thought that was your department."

Despite his youth, the doctor had backbone, Anderson decided.

"If I may continue…"

Anderson nodded his acknowledgement of the rebuke.

"She is suffering from shock and our best guess is that there must have been some sort of trauma as she's unable, or unwilling, to speak for now. When we asked her what had happened to her, she simply shook her head as if she didn't know."

"Do you think she'll remember anything?"

"It's doubtful in the short term, but her memory should come back. Slowly, mind. Her brain will probably be blocking the experience until she is better able to cope with the memories."

"Anything physically wrong with her?"

"There's no bruising on her torso, legs and arms that we could see, it appears there are no broken bones, nor any breaks that have healed and no obvious sexual trauma."

Anderson nodded, relieved. "There's lots of 'no's' in there, Doc, anything positive that we can use to try and find out what happened to her?"

"Well, she was very dehydrated and with a low blood count, with evidence of needle marks on the back of both hands."

"Needle marks?"

"Yes, um, it seems that she could have had, um, cannula's in her hands."

Ah, Anderson realised they were now getting to the nitty gritty of the case and what could be the source of the Doctor's nervousness. "What? Like you use to give a patient an anaesthetic?"

The doctor nodded. "Definitely. She was certainly given some sort of relaxant at any rate. But the marks are quite large and the back of both hands are bruised."

"Which means?"

"They have been there for some time. So, um, coupled with the dehydration and low blood count…" sweat was forming on the Doctor's brow which he wiped away, messing up his gelled hair in the process.

"Yes?" There was definitely something strange coming, Anderson could see a pulse beating on the Doctor's temple.

"I think someone has been taking her blood. Draining it from her body via her hands. I've never seen anything like it."

Anderson thought that he hadn't either. No wonder young Dr McAllister had been nervous about telling him that strange piece of news and why the nurse had been unwilling to talk to him.

Why on earth would someone want to drain a child's blood? The very thought of it was too horrific to contemplate. This was certainly shaping up to be one of his strangest cases yet. He wondered what Crane would make of it?

Seven

Diane Chambers sat opposite DI Anderson in his cubbyhole of an office, filled with files spilling off chairs, his desk and bookcases; a waterfall of paper. The space never changed and Diane wondered every time she visited Anderson, if he'd have had a clear-out. So far she'd been disappointed. His tweed jacket was slung over the back of his chair and their cups of tea were accompanied by two caramel biscuits, much to Diane's delight as she'd missed breakfast that morning.

"Diane, I need your help," Anderson began.

Those few words were music to her ears. It looked like that for once she'd have a full briefing about a case from the police, instead of having to wring every single piece of information out of them. Or at least she hoped that was what was about to happen. She ran her fingers through her short, dark, curly hair, then crossed her legs and leaned in to listen.

"There's a particularly difficult and delicate case that I'm working on and it needs sensitive reporting."

"That's an interesting choice of words," said Diane, knowing full well that the local police and military were of the opinion that sensitive was the last word anyone would use to describe her reporting. Hard hitting, thought provoking, and utterly biased were just some of the descriptors usually used when talking about her articles. But sensitive? Not so much and the thought made Diane smile. "What have you got for me?"

"A young girl has been found wandering around Ash Ranges."

Anderson paused, making Diane even more interested than she was already. Stories about children sold newspapers and in the age of on-line free news, she was constantly on the look-out for dynamic stories that would sell paper copies of the Aldershot News.

"And?"

"And we don't know who she is or where she's come from."

"Blimey," Diane said. "So what do you want from me?"

"We were hoping you'd do a bit of a spread to help us identify the girl."

Inside Diane was doing a jig of happiness, whilst trying to keep her face fairly neutral. A great story was being handed to her on a plate, what could be better? "Together with an editorial comment?"

Anderson paused for a moment, as though he were considering her request.

"I don't think I can do one without the other," Diane pressed.

"Let's talk about that after I give you the details."

Diane pretended to give consideration to this suggestion, tapping the end of her pencil against her teeth. Even though Diane always recorded any interviews on her mobile phone, she still liked the security of pencil and paper. The thought that her phone may get stolen, or broken thus losing valuable information, was too awful to contemplate, but not outside the realms of possibility. As Chief Reporter for the Aldershot News, and having climbed the ladder of the local newspaper world, she couldn't afford to make any mistakes.

Over the years she had applied for a few jobs on national newspapers, but found that once there she would have been a junior, treated like a numpty who didn't know anything, a small fish in a big pond. In Aldershot she was a big fish in a small pond, a state of affairs much more to her liking. Her eye was on the job of Deputy Editor of the newspaper group, which was currently held by a crabby man who was due to retire in six months and she was determined that her name would soon be on the door of his office.

After nodding her agreement to Anderson, he then outlined the case, which proved to be even more interesting than Diane had first thought.

"So, just to make it perfectly clear," said Diane when Anderson finished. "There is a girl who you need to identify. But equally important you also need the marks on her arms explained."

"Yes, we're hoping that someone may have seen such symbols before, or know someone who has those symbols on them."

"What do the police think they are?"

Anderson didn't reply.

"Come on, Derek, you must have some idea."

"We aren't commenting on the symbols."

Diane pulled the photographs closer to her and mulled them over. Why would someone do that? What did they mean? "Is that an upside down cross?" she asked, pointing to something near the top of the girl's left arm.

"I have no idea," Anderson said.

"Are you sure?" Diane looked at him closely. "It seems to me that some of these marks are familiar. Look at this one. Isn't it a pentagram?"

But Anderson still refused to look at the symbol she was pointing at. Which told her far more than any words could. As she wasn't sure how far she could push him, she didn't say anything else about the strange symbols on the girl's arms, but she now had an angle for her editorial piece. After all she couldn't ignore a potential case of Devil worship in Aldershot.

Eight

Crane clumped his way into the sitting room. "That was a lovely dinner, Tina," he said. "I've loaded the dishwasher."

"Um, thanks," she replied, trying to give the impression that she was caught-up in the latest episode of one of the many soap operas she watched.

She glanced up as Crane lowered himself gingerly into an armchair next to the settee where she was sitting. As she'd anticipated he started looking for a distraction from what he always described as 'the boringly over-acted dramas that were so far from the truth it was laughable'. She heard the rustle of paper and smiled as he had obviously grabbed the local newspaper that she had deliberately placed on the table next to his chair, left open at a large article talking about a girl that had been found wandering in the woods, written by his nemesis Diane Chambers, which she hoped would interest him.

As she settled into the settee while he read the paper, she glanced around the cosy sitting room. The yellow and terracotta fabric three piece suite contrasted nicely with the warm cream walls. A rusty red rug covered the beige carpet in the middle of the room and a restored Victorian fireplace with beautiful hand painted tiles was the focal point. It was so very different from their modern 3 bed detached house on the Garrison. After Tom had had his accident and was out of the army, they'd had to give up their Garrison property and had moved back into their own house in Ash, just outside of Aldershot. Luckily the contract they'd had with a family who were renting the house had been about to expire, so Tina and Tom decided it was best not to renew it and move back home.

She was glad to be back, even if Tom wasn't. Not that he hated the house, he didn't. He hated being out of the army. But for Tina it was good to have her own things around her and she was particularly pleased that her garden had survived the rental. Nearly 100' long it was split into sections, a lawn area, a play area and a vegetable plot at the end. Daniel was loving it already, taking particular delight in running up and down the length of it on his still toddler-chubby legs.

She was back at work at a local bank, which had done wonders for her self-esteem and Daniel was going to a day-nursery. They'd talked about Crane looking after Daniel at home but what with physiotherapy and rehabilitation and him being unable to get around nimbly, it seemed best to keep Daniel out of the house during the day.

As Crane grunted at something in the article, Tina said, "Diane Chambers strikes again eh?"

"What?"

"I said it is yet another inflammatory article by Diane Chambers." Tina pushed her dark, straight hair behind her ears as she looked at her husband. Her long locks had been chopped off into a short bob ending just above her shoulders. Much more practical for a busy working mother.

"Bloody stupid woman," Crane grumbled. "Just look at that headline – Devil Worship Comes to Aldershot. She does far more harm than good. Derek needs to be more careful when dealing with her."

"Oh, so you think its Derek Anderson's case then?"

"Probably, but whatever," he shrugged.

"Intriguing, though, don't you think?"

"What?"

"That poor girl. I wonder where she came from? What could have happened to her?"

Crane folded the newspaper and put it back on the table.

"So you're not interested then? Not even a little bit?" Tina pressed.

"Jesus, Tina, don't you understand yet? I'm out! No more investigating. No more army. No more Aldershot Police. For Christ's sake," he shouted and picked up the paper and poked it at her across the space between them. "And you can stop playing your stupid games. I know what you're trying to do and it won't work."

Crane struggled out of his chair and grabbed his stick.

"Where are you going?" she asked.

"To throw away this piece of rubbish and get a beer."

As he stomped out of the room, Tina wiped her suddenly tear-filled eyes. She wasn't feeling sorry for herself, but for her proud husband, who'd had everything he held dear torn from him. She had to try and get him interested in something. She'd hoped an intriguing case would have done the trick, but it appeared not. She'd just have to think of another way. Tom wasn't getting off with it that easily. Throwing a childish tantrum and storming off was something Daniel would do and was behaviour unbecoming a Sgt Major. She grinned at the army speak. Having protested at moving to the Garrison a couple of years ago when she found out she was pregnant, she now, to her surprise, found that she missed it. The wives had turned out to be good company and proved to be good friends when she'd needed them most and had been diagnosed with post natal depression after Daniel's birth. So she did understand her husband's pain, both physical and mental. There had to be a way forward for him and she was determined to find it. Maybe it was time for a phone call to Derek Anderson.

Nine

Standing outside the Victorian terrace that housed his friend and latter-day partner in crime detection, Anderson paused, taking deep breaths to prepare himself for whatever mood Crane was in. He had never given up on Crane, no matter the bad moods, the shouting or the abuse thrown at him. He understood that the accident must have been an almighty blow to his friend. It came without warning and as a result it seemed that Crane couldn't come to terms with it. With determination in every step Anderson walked up to the rich red door and grabbed the brass lion knocker, rapping it firmly. As he heard Crane thumping his way to the door, he arranged his features into a positive smile; a smile that waivered when he saw Crane's face. Dark clouds seemed to cover Crane's features and it wasn't just the whiskers on his unshaven chin. His once bright, piercing blue eyes were dulled and he appeared to be clinging onto his stick as though afraid someone would steal it.

"Oh, it's you," Crane said and turned and walked back into the depths of the house, leaving the door open. Taking that as a cue to enter, Anderson followed Crane to the kitchen, after leaving the carrier bag he was carrying on the hall table.

"Make yourself useful then," Crane indicated the kettle as he struggled to sit in one of the chairs arranged around a large farmhouse-type pine table.

Pushing down his instinct to help Crane, a move he knew from past experience would only provoke, not aid, he said, "How's things?" as he filled the kettle and grabbed two cups from the cupboard. He was very familiar with Crane's kitchen, having visited many times during Crane's convalescence, whether his presence was appreciated or not.

"How do you think?" Crane grumbled.

"Same old, same old, eh?"

"Pretty much."

"How's the physiotherapy going? Is that where you've been today?" Anderson indicated Crane's blue sweat pants and white tee-shirt.

"Yes and for your information it was bloody painful."

"Yes, well it will be, but it will be worth it in the end."

Crane seemed to slip into a sullen silence as Anderson finished his chore.

"Did you see the local paper?" Anderson asked as he put the two mugs of coffee on the table.

"Why?"

"There was a big article in there by Diane Chambers about my latest case."

"Ha!" Crane barked. "It was just her usual bluster and bullshit, so I put it where it belonged, in the rubbish bin."

"But there was a kernel of truth in it as well." Anderson kept his voice light when what he really wanted to do was to shout at his friend telling him to get a grip and cheer up. "I really do have a mystery girl."

"So?" Crane grabbed his coffee and blew across the top of it before taking a tentative sip.

"So I'm hitting a bit of a brick wall. Well, a bloody big wall, actually. I've no leads, nothing."

"Can't Staff Sgt Williams help? After all he is in charge now. At least so I hear. I was told he'd got his old rank back and is in charge of my old team."

Anderson could hear the bitterness in Crane's voice, He had to try and turn his friend away from going down that particular road.

"No, it's nothing to do with Billy. We can't find a military link and no one from the Garrison has reported a child missing, so it doesn't fall within his remit. Have you seen him?"

"Who?"

"Billy, of course."

"No, why should I?"

"Because you were friends as well as colleagues."

"I taught him everything he knows. He was lucky to have worked for me."

"Exactly, so you should be proud that you've handed the Special Investigations Branch team over to such a competent soldier and investigator."

"Suppose so."

"Definitely so. Come on, Crane, you've touched many people's lives and done a lot of good."

"How do you work that one out?"

Anderson sighed inside. He seemed to have embarked on an uphill conversation and was fearful that he might say the wrong thing. As usual.

"Think of all the cases you've solved, the people you've brought to justice."

Crane didn't reply, just kept on sipping his coffee.

Anderson said, "You saved Billy and those children; caught a terrorist and a rapist; uncovered a corruption…"

Crane interrupted, "Yes, and I failed to save a child, failed to save the Colonel's wife and found the Major's wife dead."

"For God's sake, Crane, stop being so morbid."

"Why? I can be whatever the hell I want to be."

"Okay, sorry," Anderson tried to pacify Crane.

"I'm sick to death of people telling me what I should and shouldn't do and how I should feel. Alright?" Crane slammed his mug down, spilling some of the liquid onto the table. "Now look what you've made me do!"

"Let me do that," Anderson grabbed the mug and cleaned the table with some paper towels.

"You may as well go now," said Crane once the mess was cleaned up.

"Why?" Anderson asked after throwing the sodden paper into the bin.

"Because I'm sure you've got lots to do, most of which is more important than sitting here with me, such as working on your mystery girl case, that I'm not in the least bit interested in. And anyway I've got to take my tablets and it's time for my rest."

"You sure?" Anderson got a glare in reply. "Alright, I'll be off then. Take care and I'll be back soon."

"Oh joy," Crane shouted to Anderson's back as he walked down the hall.

Anderson raised his hand in goodbye, and then left the house, deliberately leaving his carrier bag behind.

Ten

Blake put his hands on either side of his back and bent forwards and backwards, trying to loosen the knots in his spine from leaning over and decorating human flesh all day. He pulled the latex ink-spattered gloves off his hands and began to tidy up his workspace. The last punter had just left and his wife, Mimi, was locking up. His feet were killing him and he was sure she'd bought him the wrong sized boots, even though she insisted she hadn't, and his jeans were falling off him as he'd forgotten to put on a belt that morning. All in all he was glad the day was over.

Walking over to the reception desk of his shop, Totland Tattoos, Blake saw the local paper open on the counter. He scanned the headline, Devil Worship Comes To Aldershot and grinned. He was well used to the overblown articles that periodically appeared in the paper. He skim-read the several column inches devoted to the story. Apparently a young girl had been found, nearly naked, wandering around on Ash Ranges. It seemed she was unable to speak, so the police had no idea who she was. He didn't recognise her, so he didn't bother to read the rest.

"Seen the paper?" Mimi called from the back room where she was making tea.

"Yeah, why?"

Mimi appeared, carrying two mismatched cups without saucers. "They want to know about some of the marks on the girl."

"What marks?" Blake drew the paper to him once again.

Mimi put the cups down and pointed to a picture that accompanied the article. "Those ones."

Blake was glad he hadn't yet picked up his tea, as he would certainly have dropped it in shock.

"You alright?" Mimi asked. "You've gone all pale."

"I did it."

"You did what?" she asked, pushing her wild blond curls out of her eyes.

"See that sign?"

"Yeah."

"Well, I put it on a bloke a couple of months ago."

"Never!"

"I'm sure I did."

"Right," Mimi said and turned over her mobile phone which was sat next to her cup. "Best call the coppers then."

"Whoa, hold on a minute, girl," Blake said.

"Why? Look it says here you can call the Crime Stoppers line in complete confidence."

"But why should I help the coppers? Don't forget that most of our clients are, shall we say, not good friends with the police." Blake shivered in his thin black tee-shirt sporting a large picture of the rock band Metallica, at the horrific thought of losing his shop. "If they get wind of the fact that I'm helping the police, then it could be the end of the business."

"Don't be so stupid," she said. "You have to do something. Look at the picture of that poor child? How can you not help find out what happened to her? And anyway, isn't there some law or other about perverting the course of justice?"

"Don't be so daft, woman."

"I'm not being daft, Blake. What happens if they find out you were involved and you hadn't told them first?"

"Involved? I'm not bloody involved. I had nothing to do with anything. All I did was put a bloody tattoo on some bloke's arm."

"Well, its best you tell them that first isn't it, before they find out for themselves."

"Oh bloody hell, alright, but mark my words they'll want to come and interview us and I don't want them coming when we're open."

Blake ran his hands over his shaven head and absently scratched at the scab of a new tattoo on his neck as he contemplated an un-wanted meeting with the police. But the bloody woman was right, he supposed. If it had been anyone other than Mimi telling him what to do, he would have protested and won. But she was too determined, too forthright and he loved her for it. For without those qualities they wouldn't have the shop and a very nice living thank you very much. So, out of love for his wife, he supposed he'd better go along with it.

Eleven

Crane did indeed take his tablets, after Anderson had left. There were less of them to take throughout the day than when he'd first been allowed home from hospital, but there were still enough to make him rattle three times a day. But he was glad of the oblivion they brought, allowing him some respite from the pain, giving him a chance to sleep and recharge his batteries before Tina and Daniel returned home in the late afternoon.

Putting the boxes of tablets back in the kitchen cabinet, Crane grabbed his stick and made his way through the hall towards the stairs. As he passed the small table near the front door where he and Tina always left their door and car keys, he saw a plastic carrier bag that hadn't been there that morning. It must have been left by Anderson. Opening the top of the bag and looking inside he saw there was an Aldershot Police file in there. Fucking hell, he thought, that stupid bastard Anderson. Well it can bloody well stay there, he decided and let go of the bag. With renewed determination he tackled the stairs. By the time he arrived at the top, he was gasping in pain and fell on the bed with a sigh of relief. But it took some time before he was able to force his body to relax completely and the medication kicked in.

That was usually the point at which he fell asleep, but although he'd managed to relax his body, his mind was still flitting about all over the place. On the one hand he was cross that Tina and Derek seemed to be in cahoots, what with both of them trying to get him interested in Derek's latest case. But on the other, he couldn't rid himself of the image of that poor girl. She kept popping up in his mind, just as she was doing now. When he closed his eyes, he saw her; those soft brown eyes that seemed to be looking directly into his, with a steady gaze that wouldn't be deflected.

Struggling to sit up, he propped himself up on his pillows and thought he would read for a while. He didn't need to sleep, just rest on top of the bed. Reaching for his book, he saw a copy of the Aldershot News again, this time placed on top of his books. For God's sake, Tina wasn't giving up. She must have rescued the paper from the bin and left it there for him before she went to work that morning. He decided it could bloody well stay there and he pulled his book from underneath it.

Opening it he found his place and started to read. But for some reason his favourite topic of military history wasn't cutting it and his mind kept wandering back to Tina, Anderson and the girl, so in the end he gave in. Thrusting the book to one side he picked up the newspaper, reading once again about the unknown child and the strange marks on her arm.

Throwing the paper down onto the bed he decided a cup of something was in order and made his painful way back to the kitchen, where he brewed a cup of tea. Propped up against the work surface he took a few tentative sips, but the tea was still too hot to drink properly, so he took it through to the lounge with him, wondering if there was any cricket on the television. As he walked through the hall he once more spied Anderson's carrier bag, which he studiously ignored.

He put his tea down on a side table and turned on the television, flicking through the channels. But as he couldn't find anything worth watching, he settled for the news. He listened to the sports report about how the cricket had just finished (England were losing as usual), the latest FA Cup news (he was looking forward to watching the Reading v Chelsea match on Friday night) and Indian Wells tennis was due to start that week end (would Andy Murray be able to beat Djokovic this time?). As the local news headlines started he was confronted with the picture of the girl. Yet again. This time her face filled the television screen.

He thought about the newspaper article...

He thought about the file sitting on the hall table that Derek had left...

He guessed it wouldn't hurt to take a look. Not that he was going to help. Not that he was going to get involved. No way.

Twelve

"You fucking idiot, how could you have lost the bloody girl!"

Clay looked at the boss, who was incandescent with rage. His face was red, his ginger hair standing on end, spittle flew from his lips, his fists were bunched and he took a threatening step towards Clay, who was feeling decidedly nervous. He felt like cringing and curling up into a ball in a dark corner, but decided to try and find some backbone and go on the attack, rather than the defence. He'd read somewhere that that was the best course of action, the one that was least expected.

"Look, it's alright," Clay said, raking his fingers through his long hair. "According to the paper she hasn't said a word. Nothing. Can't. They say she's too traumatised to speak."

"Well you'd better hope she stays that way."

At last the boss seemed to be calming down, his voice had quietened and his breathing was beginning to return to normal. He no longer looked as though he were going to have a heart attack.

"In the meantime we need another one. Spring equinox is coming up so you'd better have a suitable girl by then. You know what to do. Same procedure as last time."

"Alright, alright," Clay jabbered with relief and put out his hands palms up. It appeared he'd got away with it.

"And you don't want to know what the penance will be if you don't. So no more fuck ups. Do we understand each other?"

Realising he still wasn't out of the woods, Clay thought that a bit of grovelling was called for, "Yes, boss, of course, boss," he said as the man walked off, climbed into a new Lexus and drove away slowly, the car tipping and rolling over the bumpy earth outside the abandoned Nissen huts.

Glad to be dismissed, but grumbling under his breath, Clay walked to his small van. It was alright for some, he thought, driving around in a new car and giving everyone orders. Why couldn't he have been the successful one? Sometimes life just wasn't fair. But then thinking about his lifestyle, he realised that a change in his fortunes was never going to happen. He was just too plain lazy and liked a smoke of weed every now and then. Well every night if he was honest. Maybe that's what was slowing him down. Turning on the ignition, the engine of his van turned over sluggishly, before settling into a noisy tick over. The exhaust was on its last legs, and he was sure the engine wasn't too clever either, it sounded more like a diesel than a petrol van. But Clay didn't have any money to fix it. He supposed the exhaust would fall off one of these days, but hopefully not before he'd driven North, found and abducted a suitable girl and made it back to Farnborough.

He trusted he'd get paid for this new girl and not be financially penalised by the boss in a fit of anger. It wasn't his bloody fault the boss had selected an old, abandoned house in the middle of nowhere, with rotten wood and rusty bolts, for their Satanic meetings. It was no wonder the girl had escaped. He ignored the little voice in the back of his head that said he hadn't locked the doors behind him that night, when he'd been spooked by her turning on him. He'd hated to see her cry and then when she'd shouted at him to get out, he sort of panicked and ran. He daren't ever mention that to the boss. He dreaded to think what the repercussions would be.

Thinking about it, perhaps he should have kept her drugged more, but it didn't seem right, pumping her full of shit, and he'd been afraid that she might overdose and die. And that would have been on him. No way was he killing anyone. He might do a few dodgy deals and be a muscle for hire, but he drew the line at killing. Especially killing kids.

Swinging the van onto the main road, Clay settled in for a long journey. But then as he checked his rear-view mirror he glimpsed himself in it. He saw his hair was unruly and curling over his shoulders. He had the start of a straggly beard. His clothes looked as greasy and grimy as his hair and when he sniffed his arm pits, he wished he hadn't.

Nah, he thought, best go home first and clean up, as otherwise he'd have no luck with the kids. They'd all be too frightened of him.

Thirteen

Anderson pushed through the people blocking the automatic glass doors at the entrance to Frimley Park Hospital. At eleven in the morning, the hospital was chock full of in-patients, out-patients, visitors and their families and he felt like a rugby scrum-half running the gauntlet of the opposing team as he tried to score a vital touch-down. He tripped over a pram wheel and would have fallen to the floor if a pair of strong arms hadn't caught him.

"You alright, Derek?" a familiar voice asked.

Anderson looked up to see that his saviour was none other than Tom Crane. After retrieving Crane's stick from the floor and handing it over, Derek said, "Thanks for that. What are you doing here?"

"Just finished physiotherapy," Crane said and rubbed at his hip. "Bloody bloke will be the death of me. I'm just going to have a coffee and a bit of a rest before I go back home."

"Excellent idea," said Anderson. "I'll join you."

Anderson carried their purchases on a tray over to an empty table overlooking a garden area, which was nothing more than a bit of scrub grass and a sad looking willow tree. Not the enticing peaceful place it should have been for those wishing to get away from the humdrum of the hospital and perhaps reflect on a particular problem, Anderson thought. And a Weeping Willow wasn't the smartest of choices for a centre-piece tree, especially for the newly bereaved. He brushed aside his thoughts of the garden and placed the tray on the table.

"Thanks," said Crane sitting down and swallowing a pain killer with a swig from a bottle of water. "What are you doing here anyway?" he asked.

"Oh, I'm just about to see that child. You know, my mystery girl."

"She's still in hospital then?"

"Yeah. To be honest we don't know what else to do with her. The last thing I want to do is to hand her over to social services in case she becomes even more traumatised by being moved and sent to a children's home or foster parents." Anderson paused to take a bite from his sugar coated doughnut. "Mm," he grimaced. "It's a bit stale," and he was forced to take a gulp of coffee to make the cake go down.

"How is she?"

Anderson thought he saw a sliver of interest in Crane's eyes. Wiping sugar off his hands with a napkin, he said, "Still not talking. To be honest I don't know what to do. I could really do with another take on the case, but I can't find anyone interested enough to help me."

He paused and raised his eyebrows at Crane, wondering if his friend would comment on the fact that he had left the file at his house. As Crane didn't bite, he continued, "You would have thought the fact that it's a child involved would melt even the hardest of hearts."

"It does seem a strange case," Crane said, gulping down the dregs of his coffee and collecting his belongings.

Disappointed at the lack of an offer of help from Crane, Anderson said, "Anyway I better be off as well," throwing his scrunched up napkin into his empty cup in frustration.

At the doors of the café, Anderson went to turn left towards the wards. He raised his hand in a gesture of good-bye, but hesitated when Crane didn't turn away from him.

"I, um, could do with trying to loosen this hip up a bit," said Crane. "Maybe I could walk up to the ward with you? The exercise would do me good."

***

Crane and Anderson stood by the door of the child's room, looking in through the glass panels. As if sensing their presence, the girl turned her head and stared directly at them. Her large eyes seemed even more mesmerising in the flesh than in the newspaper photograph and Crane had trouble tearing his gaze away. The poor kid. He wondered what on earth she had been through to end up in this state? Why was no one looking for her? He couldn't help draw a parallel between her and his son Daniel; a child who lived in a happy home, full of love.

As the girl looked away, Crane noticed a young woman sat by the side of the child's bed. "Who's she?" Crane asked.

"A young policewoman, a Family Liaison Officer. I particularly requested she not be in uniform as I thought that might be too frightening for the girl. She sits and holds her hand, reads to her, plays songs; anything to try and get a reaction, but so far nothing."

Not wishing to go in and upset the child, Crane waited outside while Anderson entered the room and talked to the young FLO. The child's arms were outside the bed covers and Crane looked at the strange symbols painted on them. It was difficult to see the individual ones from that distance, but he wondered at the mental torture of seeing something painted on your arms that you didn't want, and didn't understand what they were or why they were there.

Anderson interrupted Crane's introspection as he left the room and joined him. "Are they tattooed on?" Crane asked, pointing at the girl's arms.

"No, they're henna apparently, so they will fade with time, thank God. She doesn't need to have a permanent reminder of whatever the hell they did with her."

Crane nodded in agreement.

Scrabbling in his pocket, Anderson retrieved his mobile which was ringing and walked off while he took the call. Returning, he said to Crane, "That was the office. Apparently a tattoo artist has come forward. He recognised one of the symbols. So I need to go and see him. Now." Anderson paused. "Well?" he asked, jangling his keys in his trouser pocket.

Crane let the question hang for a moment. Closing his eyes he saw again the girl's stare, her dark eyes seemingly pleading with him to help her. Opening his own eyes he said, "Well, I think that as I could do with a lift home, maybe I could come with you to see the tattoo artist and afterwards you could drop me back at my house. What do you think?"

Fourteen

Anderson pulled up outside a tattoo shop set in a row of shops on the Totlands Estate, on the outskirts of Farnborough. Crane clambered awkwardly out of the car and stood looking at the outside of the shop. There was a glass door in the middle of two large windows which sported various tattoos mounted on pieces of card. But the photographs were old, fading and curling off their backings. From the outside the whole shop had an air of desolation about it, reflecting the estate it was situated in.

Crane could see a middle-aged man wearing a dark tee-shirt and jeans, stood behind a counter near the front of the shop. His arms appeared completely covered in tattoos, in what Crane thought was called 'a sleeve'. He guessed you had to be interested in tattoos to become keen enough to train as an artist.

Anderson joined him at the door. "Ready?" he asked.

"Ready," Crane grinned for the first time in many months. He felt a bubble of excitement in the pit of his stomach, worming its way up through his body. Supressing his eagerness, he followed Anderson into the shop. The inside smelled a bit musty, intermingled with an undercurrent of stale sweat, and looked as dilapidated as the outside. But Crane could see empty booths that were spotlessly clean and organised. It seemed the attention to detail didn't extend to the waiting area of the shop.

Crane stood silently next to the policeman, while Derek showed his credentials and told the man why they were there.

"Do we have to do this now?" the man who had introduced himself as Blake said.

"Yes we do," Anderson replied.

"It's just that the customers won't like it. You know, the police being in here."

"What customers are those then?" Anderson asked looking around the empty shop.

Outmanoeuvred, Blake had no choice but to answer Anderson's questions.

"Can you firstly explain what happens when someone comes into the shop for a tattoo?"

Blake told them that he took the customer's details down; name, address and phone number. Then they talked about what sort of tattoo the customer wanted and where it was to be placed on the body.

"Some know what they want," Blake said, "Others don't and need some guidance, hence the books of tattoos," and Blake pointed to three large ring binders on a low coffee table placed in front of a row of dilapidated chairs. One of which Crane sank gratefully into.

"How come you tattooed this particular symbol?" Anderson asked. "Is it is in one of those books there?"

"No, I checked at the time," Blake replied. "It wasn't something that I'd done before. The bloke brought in a piece of paper with the symbol drawn on it and I had to do it freehand."

"Freehand? What does that mean?"

Blake went on to explain that most tattoo artists used a template and drew over it, like kids in school making a copy on tracing paper and then transferring that onto another piece of paper or into a book.

"That's what we do, but we transfer it directly onto the customer's skin, that's for the ones that we already have designs for. This one was different. I had to draw it on the bloke's arm freehand and then tattoo over the design. There aren't many of us that do the freehand stuff and I've got a bit of a reputation for it."

"I'll need the customer's details," Anderson said.

"Well, there's the problem," he said. "The missus said that you'd want them and made me look for them. But the truth is that I can't remember when he came in, so I can't pinpoint the customer."

"So you don't make a note of which customer had which tattoo?"

"Sorry. There's no need for me to do that. I'm afraid I can't help you."

Crane could see the frustration in Anderson's face as the lead turned out to be a dead end. As Crane rose with the help of his stick, Anderson said, "If the same man comes back, or anyone else wants this symbol or something similar…"

"Yes, I get it, I'll call you."

"Good." Anderson slid his card over the counter. "In the meantime could you describe the man you tattooed?"

"Well, I do that many, they all run into one another you know? But the thing I remember about this bloke is that he had ginger hair."

"Anything else? Beard? Other tattoos? Clothes?"

"No, sorry, I just remember ginger hair and fair skin with freckles."

Fifteen

As Anderson drove them back, Crane was particularly quiet, but this time in a good way, not because he was in a bad mood, which was his usual emotional state. Crane was beginning to realise that for the first time in a long time his leg hadn't hurt for a while. Thinking back, the last time had been when he had come out of the physiotherapy suite earlier that morning. He stretched his leg out as much as he could in the foot-well of the passenger side of Anderson's Ford Focus, rubbing his hip as he did so. He was wearing a track suit and trainers at the insistence of his personal therapist, or rather his personal sadist, who wanted him to wear comfortable loose clothing and stable footwear for their sessions. The man was worse than any physical training instructor Crane had ever encountered in the army. A brutal taskmaster, who if he thought that Crane wasn't trying hard enough, would deliberately let the session run over until he was satisfied that Crane was putting in as much effort as he could.

The morning had been a welcome change of routine for Crane who had, for so long, missed the company of Anderson and the case had given them the chance to talk about something other than his accident. He wondered now why he had been so hesitant before, been so deliberately dismissive of Tina and Anderson's efforts to get him interested in the case and realised that it was down to his fear. Fear that his body wouldn't be up to anything more than mooching around the house and fear that his brain had become as slow and sluggish as his leg. He realised that by taking away the fear, he had taken away the anger that had been an integral part of him since the accident.

But just because he'd had a good morning, did it mean he'd be able to take an active part in an investigation? Crane wasn't a stupid man. He understood that at the moment he could no longer chase criminals, run after them, tackle and take them down. But maybe, just maybe there was a small role for him. One that would enable him to feel like a useful human being again.

Just then a twinge of pain reminded Crane that the gremlins were still there, still burrowing away in his hip joint, but what he had managed to do was to think of something else for an hour or two, instead of focusing on his injury.

After he got out of the car, he leaned back in through the open door and said, "Let me know if anything else happens with the case will you? If there are any new developments?"

"Will do," said Anderson with a broad grin on his face that Crane just about managed not to match. He didn't want Anderson thinking that he was about to become Crane's personal saviour. He'd never live it down and Anderson would become insufferable.

Before driving off, Anderson opened the window and shouted, "Oh and if you have any thoughts about the case, give me a ring? Please?"

Crane didn't answer, just waved goodbye in reply as he walked up to his front door. Once in, Crane took off his coat and hung it in the small cloakroom where their winter coats, boots and all of Daniel's outdoor stuff was stored. He noticed the police file that he'd meant to give back to Anderson, was still resting on the hall table. Waiting for him. Glad now that he hadn't handed it back, Crane took it into the kitchen with him. He was fully aware that he'd not actually contributed anything towards the case this morning. It was as if he'd been struck dumb. Perhaps if he read through the file it would help him contribute to the conversation next time. If there was to be a next time.

Deciding to make a cup of tea, he stood before the boiling kettle scratching at his beard. It wasn't as short as it normally was. Crane hadn't much bothered about shaving, it hadn't been high on his list of priorities. His hair had grown longer as well and was now curling all over the place. If he didn't keep it short it just sprouted curls which seemed to grow and multiply as fast as weeds. Perhaps he'd fit in a visit to the barbers when he was next in town.

But for now he wanted to study the close up photographs of those strange marks on the girl's arms.

Sixteen

To be honest, Bethany was a bit fed up of people looking at her, poking her and prodding her. She just wanted her mum and dad. But she couldn't seem to tell anyone. Somehow her voice didn't work anymore and she didn't know why. It was just too hard to form words, too hard to wake her voice up, too hard to think about anything apart from wanting to go home.

She didn't know how she'd got to the hospital, didn't know why she was there. There were vague memories playing around in the back of her head, like early morning mist. But just like mist when she tried to grab it in her hand, it just… disappeared. And she'd fall asleep and then start the whole thing over again when she woke up.

They seemed to be calling her Hope. She'd no idea why, for her name was the one thing she did know. It was Bethany. But she couldn't seem to tell them that either. There was a woman sat with her most of the time. At first Bethany had thought that the woman was there to stop her if she tried to run away from the hospital, just like she'd… she'd… oh bother, she'd lost it again. There had been a wisp of something, a half memory, a thought that perhaps she'd run away from somewhere else before. But no… there was nothing else.

Victoria. That was the woman's name. She brought in books to read out loud and had given her a mobile phone to play games on. She could have used it to phone her mum, Victoria said, which she would have done if she could only remember the number. Sometimes they'd watch the TV together, but never the news, only cartoons and stuff. Victoria didn't seem to mind that she didn't talk to her. But Bethany now trusted Victoria enough to nod her head in answer to a question, or gave her a little smile when she did something kind, like bringing in a chocolate bar or some sweets. But somehow she didn't have any appetite. She seemed to have lost it, just as she'd lost the ability to speak, just like she'd lost the ability to remember anything.

The whole thing was so scary that Bethany decided it was easier and less frightening to close her eyes and sleep.

***

On the recommendation of the hospital, Anderson had arranged for a child psychologist to work with the girl who had been dubbed, Hope, instead of calling her 'the child' or 'the girl', all phrases which seemed to detach her emotionally from the team working on trying to find out who she was. And so Operation Hope was in full swing. Teams of officers, including cadets drafted in from the nearest police training college and members of the military police, were combing the area of Ash Ranges where she had been found. But it was a hopeless job really, as the ranges sprawled over several miles. Anderson wasn't even sure what they expected to find, or were even looking for. He didn't know if Hope had run away from a nearby house (not that there were many) or if someone had dumped her there (in which case she could have been held many miles away). So really their only expectation was to get some information from Hope herself.

Anderson was waiting outside Hope's room when a smartly dressed, slim woman walked towards him down the corridor. Her business suit was charcoal grey, teamed with a white blouse and her dark hair was severely drawn back from her face. Her black framed glasses gave her a studious air and all in all Anderson thought that her appearance was rather frightening.

"DI Anderson?" she asked, extending her hand. "Dr McAllister."

"Thank you for coming," Anderson said, but looking at the woman he wondered how the hell she was supposed to relate to Hope.

"I've been given what background you have on the child," she said, "and I'm going to use drawing therapy first, to try and get some information that you can work with."

"Thank you," Anderson said. "How long does it usually take? I mean, how many sessions would you recommend?"

"Well, it's not an exact science, you know, but I'll do what I can as quickly as I can. That's about the best I can say, really. I'll call in at least once a day, but I don't want to rush her or frighten her."

Anderson thought that Dr McAllister would definitely seem rather frightening to Hope, as she came across as rather frosty and unnervingly professional and so he was unprepared for what she did next. She took off her jacket and pulled her blouse out of the waistband of her skirt. Then she grabbed the pins that were taming her hair, pulled them out and ran her fingers through the curls, allowing them to fall to her shoulders. She grabbed her large handbag which was bulging with her files and took out a sketch pad and a tin of crayons. She swapped her high heeled shoes for a flat pair that were folded up in her bag. Her glasses went into a case and joined the shoes in her bag.

"Right," she said. "That's better, don't you think?" and without waiting for a stunned Anderson to reply, she pushed open the door to Hope's room.

Seventeen

Anderson couldn't resist calling in on Crane on his way back to the police station, to tell him about the psychologist.

"It was a real transformation," he said sitting in Crane's kitchen, enjoying a cup of tea and one of the muffins that Tina had bought especially for his visits. She knew all about Derek's sweet tooth and even though his wife Jean had banned Tina from assisting with Anderson's ever growing waistline, Tina always seemed to take pity on him and made sure there were little treats in the cupboard for him.

"When Dr McAllister first arrived, she frightened me to death, and I was about to suggest that maybe drawing therapy wasn't the way forward. But she turned out to be so different from my preconceptions. I've never seen anything like it."

"So how did Hope react to her?"

"Well, so far Dr McAllister has only managed to get her to draw the doctor. They played a game of drawing each other, which brought a smile to Hope's face and it was the first time I have seen her animated. And the first time she's actually joined in an activity."

"Were you or the FLO involved?"

"No, we stayed outside and watched through the window.

"Um, interesting," said Crane. "Has she left the drawing materials with Hope?"

"No, she says that could do more harm than good. She thinks it's best that she explores things with Hope while she draws, as the therapy needs to be done under controlled circumstances for now. That way Dr McAllister can tease out any memories without Hope getting too upset, or feeling pressured by someone asking her a lot of questions about what she's drawn."

"Sounds fair enough. I guess that will help if anything she draws or tells you, is eventually used in evidence."

"That's exactly what Dr McAllister said. If she's in charge of the therapy then we can't be accused of putting words into Hope's mouth or giving her ideas to fit whatever theories we may come up with about her abduction and captivity." Anderson took another bite of his muffin. "These really are good," he said through a mouthful of crumbs. "Chocolate muffins with chocolate chips are my favourite."

"When is Dr McAllister going to see Hope next?" Crane asked in what he hoped was a casual tone as he cleared away their cups and plates.

"Why's that?" Derek asked as he brushed crumbs off his jacket, managing to smear chocolate on his tie in the process.

"Oh, I just thought that maybe I could come as well. Just to observe you know."

"Oh sure," laughed Anderson. "Just to observe. In that case, I'll pick you up at 9am tomorrow morning. Unless you've got anything better to do, that is."

"Funnily enough, my calendar isn't overflowing with

social engagements, so 09:00 hours it is," said Crane, feeling as excited as a school boy about to go on a visit to a theme park.

As he closed the door on Anderson, his exuberance started to evaporate, as fear tried to poke holes into the thin fabric of his good mood. Turning away from the door he decided to log onto the internet. A search for lost memory as a result of trauma, would be a good place to start. And then he could look up drawing therapy. He looked at his watch and wondered how much work he'd be able to get done before Tina and Daniel came home.

Eighteen

Clay had arrived in Birmingham last evening and had spent the night camped out in his van, lying on blankets and zipped into a sleeping bag. Crawling out of the stuffy claustrophobic space, his feet touched the tarmac and he stood up, uncurling himself vertebrae by vertebrae as each clicked back into place. He groaned with pain. A nice hot bath or shower would do him right about now, but he knew he would have to get by with a wash at a local café. If only the boss hadn't been so stingy, he could have stayed in a bed and breakfast or motel somewhere close by, but the bastard wouldn't hear of it.

"You need to be seen by as few people as possible," he'd said. "I can't have you staying somewhere. What if the police mount an operation in the area and some dippy landlady recognises you? No, the van it is," he'd said firmly.

Clay thought it an excuse for not spending money, but on the other hand he was too frightened of the boss to not do as he was told.

The man he called the boss, had appeared in the area about three months ago, and started making tentative enquiries in the local alternative scene, for anyone who might be interested in setting up a new chapter. At first Clay had thought he'd meant motorbikes, but it soon became apparent that the boss had far more devilish things in mind. Clay was all for trying something new; anything that pierced the boredom of his life on the dole was welcome. He'd quickly become immersed in the new Satanic chapter and as he had a lot of time on his hands he was soon given the responsibility of sourcing the materials they needed for what the boss called, 'the worship'. Clay didn't give a damn who they worshipped, God or the Devil; it was all the same to him. What it had done was to give him a new purpose in life, a new focus, and it had also meant that he'd made a few quid on the side too.

But all that didn't improve his current mood and muttering and grumbling under his breath, he walked along the terraced streets to a local greasy spoon café. The lights were on and the windows were steamed up, which was alright by him. Walking inside was like entering a sauna and he smiled to himself. That was better. A good fry-up, some heat and a wash and he'd feel like a new man. Ready for anything. Or at least ready for any likely kid that happened to pass his way.

Once full of the breakfast special, Clay made his way to the lock up garage he'd parked near last night. Pleased to see that no one had interfered with the padlocks that secured the garage door, he managed to unlock them with a bit of a struggle, having to wiggle the keys backwards and forwards before the clasps popped open. He'd have to give them a squirt of WD40 later. The up and over door swung open on the large springs, revealing the boss' secret weapon. Climbing into the driver's seat, Clay started the engine and slowly backed the van out of the garage, parking it at the kerbside. Once the lock-up was secured again, Clay began his preparations.

It was a couple of hours later by the time he was ready and on his way. He'd gone over the contents, made sure he had his cones and sauces and that the dispensing machine was full of newly made ice-cream. He didn't carry stocks of ice lollies for obvious reasons, just the soft ice cream that came out of his dispenser.

He drove around for a while, until he found a likely spot. Parking by the side of a local park, he watched the children and their mothers playing, hearing them tell their offspring that if they behaved themselves they could have an ice cream from the van on the way home. He did quite a bit of trade, until the customers dawdled away and only one girl was left. She appeared to be on her own with no vigilant grown up and he put her age at about 10 years old, as she had that coltish look about her, all long arms and legs. She was a skinny little thing, dressed in an odd assortment of clothes that didn't scream designer; they looked like they were more charity shop bargains.

"Hey," Clay called to her, "Want an ice cream?"

"Can't," she replied sauntering over to the window. "I don't have any money."

"Oh, that's alright," Clay said. "I'll give you one for free if you can keep a secret and not tell anyone."

A grin split her face and she nodded enthusiastically, pushing her long blond hair away from her eyes.

While carefully selecting a cone and then filling it with ice cream, he asked, "What's your name?"

"Dawn."

"That's a lovely name. Where do you live then, Dawn? How come no one's with you?"

"Oh, I'm staying at the local Dr Bernardo's Children's Home. Just temporary, like. Until my mum gets better, then I can go back home. I sort of escaped this afternoon," she giggled. "But no one will notice, as long as I'm back in time for tea."

"Well," Clay said. "I hope your mum gets better soon, Dawn. I'll tell you what, how about some of my special sauce to go on the top of this," and he showed her the large ice cream cone he'd made her.

Wide eyed she nodded her agreement.

"Would you like chocolate or strawberry?"

She chose chocolate and Clay grinned as he poured it all over the top of the ice cream..

Nineteen

The following morning Crane was ready by 08:30 hours, even though Anderson wasn't coming for another half an hour, astonishing Tina in the process. In fact he was ready so early that he was given the task of making sure Daniel ate his breakfast.

Sipping the last of her coffee, as she propped herself up against the sink in the kitchen, Tina said, "So how are you feeling today?"

"Pretty good, actually," Crane said, realising that it was true. It had taken a while for him to get going, but a hot shower had helped and dressing in a suit had made him feel that he had some sort of worth. He knew it was only a temporary assignment. For now he was just tagging along with Derek. There was nothing official about it. For a moment Crane resented that, feeling that perhaps what Anderson was organising was nothing more than a pity party; but he quickly squashed such a stupid, self-obsessed, skewed view of life. He was determined to view the exercise as a positive, rather than a negative.

"It took quite a while to get ready, mind," he continued. "I guess I'm out of practice and this stupid leg didn't help."

"Have you taken your tablets?"

He nodded his agreement as he handed Daniel a toasted soldier to stick into his boiled egg, mindful of his crisp white shirt as Daniel moved it to and fro, spraying himself with egg yolk.

At the ring of the doorbell, Crane shrugged on his suit jacket and Tina handed him his stick.

"Have a good one," she grinned.

"I'll try," he replied, smiling in return, as he made his cautious way out of the house and down the front steps.

"Well look at you!" Anderson said, opening the car door for Crane.

"I don't know what you mean, Derek, just because I've put a suit on."

"Well at least it still fits you after sitting on your arse for months."

Anderson got a swipe from Crane's stick for that remark.

Even though they'd had to crawl through the rush hour traffic, both men where in an upbeat mood when they finally arrived at Frimley Park Hospital.

Crane said, "It's a bit early for the child psychologist to be visiting Hope, isn't it?"

"She wanted to fit a session in before she started her clinic today. Anyway, everyone is woken up so early on the wards that she decided it wouldn't make any difference to Hope, who'd be wide awake."

As they walked by the hospital gift shop, Derek paused. "Hang on a minute," he said and disappeared inside.

Crane waited patiently, supporting himself with his stick, determined not to focus on the gremlins that were themselves waking up, ready for their morning assault on his hip.

As Anderson re-appeared by his side holding a paper bag, Crane said, "What's that?"

"I just thought I'd bring Hope a treat," Anderson said as they made their way to the ward.

Arriving at Hope's room, Dr McAllister saw them through the window and left Hope's bedside to join them outside. She was clutching a picture.

After Anderson introduced her to Crane she said, "Look at this, DI Anderson. Hope drew a van this morning."

"Did she say anything about it?"

"No, she still won't talk. But when I asked if she'd had a ride in a van recently she nodded. I feel its great progress. She's really taken to the drawing therapy."

"Maybe she was bundled into a van when she was abducted," Crane said.

"It's a possibility," agreed Anderson. "But we'll have to wait and see if the Doc here can get any more out of her."

"Oh, I'm sure I can, you can count on that."

Anderson smiled and said, "Well in that case, Hope really deserves this treat," and he held out his paper bag. "I got her an ice cream. We passed the shop on the ground floor when we arrived and I suddenly thought she might like one. My kids love them. Would you take it to her?"

"With pleasure," the Doctor said and disappeared inside the room.

Crane said, "Can I see the-" but that was as far as he got, as a scream emerged from Hope's room. It was rather muted, heard through the window and the closed door, but it was a scream all the same.

A stunned Crane and Anderson watched helplessly,

as Hope appeared to be throwing a tantrum. She was screaming and crying and trying to get away from the ice cream cone that Anderson had bought her and which now lay abandoned on her bed. Suddenly she grabbed it and threw it across the room before collapsing, engulfed by sobs. As Dr McAllister comforted her, Hope became calmer, while the ice cream slowly melted, pooling across the floor.

Twenty

"And she went loopy you say? Just because you gave her an ice cream?"

"Well, loopy is not the best term to use, DC Douglas," Anderson said at the team briefing he'd called after arriving back at Aldershot Police Station. "But yes, that's what she did."

Crane said, "It seems that the ice cream was definitely the trigger."

Crane had already been introduced to the team, Anderson using Crane's old rank of Sgt Major. He was already known to most of the CID members because of his involvement in previous joint military and civilian police cases. Even though the structure of the police investigative teams changed from time to time, what with the introduction of the Major Crimes squad and such like, most of the team still worked out of Aldershot. The only new faces he didn't know were DC Douglas who had just been promoted out of uniform into CID and DS Bullock who had recently transferred to Aldershot from a town somewhere in the Midlands.

"But what does it mean?" Douglas asked. "Why would she get so upset at the sight of an ice cream?"

"That's for you lot to try and work out," said Anderson.

"What about the van that she drew?" Crane asked.

"Good point, Crane. DS Bullock can you work on that one? See if you can pinpoint what sort of van it could be from her drawing."

"Sorry, guv? You really think that her drawing is accurate? We are talking about a picture drawn by a kid."

"How about an ice cream van?" DC Douglas blurted.

"What?"

"Well, Hope had a bad reaction to the ice cream and she'd already drawn a van so…"

"What rubbish," said Bullock.

"We don't know if it is or not, do we Bullock?" Anderson snapped. "But we've precious little else to work on, so you and DC Douglas better get started. See what you can find out about ice cream vans in the area."

"Yes, guv," Bullock mumbled, flushing red with embarrassment.

Crane realised that blushing was an unfortunate trait in those who had pale skin and ginger hair; when even the smallest of slight or uncomfortable situation caused the rush of blood to their skin to be immediately visible… Bloody hell. Ginger hair, pale skin and freckles. Crane had heard that description before. It had been from Blake at the tattoo shop. No surely not, it could just be co-incidence. Couldn't it? There must be ginger-haired men all over the place. It didn't mean that DS Bullock was the man who'd got the strange tattoo.

But once Crane's thinking was drawn to Bullock, he couldn't stop dwelling on it and he began to wonder if the man had any tattoos. Crane looked closely, but Bullock had his suit jacket on.

As Anderson finished handing out the assignments,

he drew the meeting to a close and Crane followed him into his office.

"I'm not sure that I'm going to get much out of that lot," Anderson sighed, throwing a file on his desk to join the other half dozen already there. "They're pretty bloody useless."

"I was thinking while you were spouting away," Crane said lowering himself into the chair opposite Anderson's desk with the aid of his stick.

"Oh yes, thinking about what?" Anderson seemed more interested in finding something to eat from his bottom draw than listening to Crane.

"About ginger haired men with pale skin, freckles and a tattoo."

Anderson froze with a packet of fig biscuits in his hand.

"Bullock?"

Crane nodded.

Anderson said, "No surely not. He's been in the force for years. It must just be pure co-incidence. Here, have a biscuit it'll help take your mind off your fantasies."

Crane took the biscuit but not the advice that came with it.

Twenty One

As Crane walked into the house, exhausted and exhilarated all at the same time from his day with Anderson, Tina and Daniel were already at home and once he'd deposited his keys on the table and taken off his coat, he walked through the house to the kitchen to meet them.

"Hey, stranger," Tina said, giving him a kiss on the cheek. "I was wondering where you were. Did you have physiotherapy at the hospital this afternoon? Only you hadn't said."

"No, I didn't, I um…"

Tina scrutinised his face. "Tom, where have you been? Are you alright? I was becoming afraid that you'd had an accident - again."

"Stop worrying, Tina," he said moving over to give her a hug and a kiss on her cheek to dispel her worries, although he was secretly pleased that she was so concerned about him. "Actually, yes I am alright, more alright than I have been in quite a while. Any tea on the go?"

"You don't get off that lightly," she said. "Although I might make you a cup once you've told me what's going on," she teased. "Could it have anything to do with Derek Anderson?"

When he didn't answer, she turned to the sink and filled the kettle with water. "So he's finally got you sufficiently interested in his case has he?" she called. Clicking on the kettle she turned back to him. "Is that where you've been all day? I thought you were just going for an hour or so to meet that woman psychologist before you went to your appointment at the pain management clinic in the same hospital. Wasn't Derek just giving you a lift?"

"Oh shit, I forgot all about that," grinned Crane and bent to pick up a toy that Daniel had dropped out of his high chair.

"Oh, Tom!"

"Don't 'oh Tom' me. It's not a problem. I'll just carry on as I am. All the tablets are on repeat prescription, so it's no bother."

"So, what it is that you were you doing that was more important than managing your pain?" Tina finished making his tea and sat down at the table, pushing the mug towards him.

He sat down opposite her. "Well, as it happens," he began, "Hope drew a van and then threw a wobbly when Derek brought her an ice-cream. So the theory is…" and Crane outlined what had happened at the team briefing earlier.

Much to his surprise, instead of berating him for being at 'work' for so long, she grinned and said, "Well I'm really pleased."

"What, that I forgot my appointment?"

"Ha ha. I mean I'm pleased that you found something interesting to do. Well done Derek is what I say. It seems his plan is working."

Crane looked closely at his wife his face, frowning. "What do you mean?" And then the penny dropped. "You mean you know all about it? What's he been saying? Are you in on this as well?"

But Tina just smiled enigmatically and getting up from the table, turned away to get Daniel's tea ready.

Twenty Two

"And so, in the name of Satan, we set your feet upon the left-hand path...Dawn we baptize you with earth and air, with brine and burning flame. And so we dedicate your life to love, to passion, to indulgence, and to Satan, and the way of darkness. Hail Dawn! Hail Satan!"

As the ritual drew to a close and he heard the nine rings of the bell, he relaxed, safe in the knowledge that it was over at last. They'd completed a successful Satanic baptism and his first major success. He looked around at the members gathered in the dilapidated ruin, squinting through the candle smoke, trying to decide which of the women to favour when it was time for the fun to begin. But he pulled himself together, as first of all he needed to speak to the couple who were to bring the child up as their own. He must make sure that they understood that she must be convinced that her new adoptive parents were offering her the best chance of a good life. She had to be persuaded that as her mother was now dead, theirs was to be her new home. Okay so that was a bit of a lie, he'd no idea if her mother was dead or not, but it would do as a suitable story.

He suddenly realised that Clay was still standing by

the altar and that he was looking at the girl with something akin to horror in his eyes.

"Clay," he shouted. "Get the girl ready to go off with her new parents."

But Clay didn't move, not even a fraction. He could have been frozen by Medusa's head.

Grumbling he strode over to the altar. "Clay," he shouted in the man's ear to get his attention. "What the hell's the matter with you?"

"I'm alright, it's her, boss!"

"What are you talking about, what about her?"

"Um, I think she's dead. I can't wake her up."

Clay looked up at him with terror in his eyes, but if it was because something had happened to the girl, or because Clay was afraid of him, he wasn't sure which.

"Oh, for God's sake, get out of the way," and he pushed Clay to one side.

Pulling off his hood so he could see properly, he looked down at the motionless girl. She should be stirring by now. Waking up. And she wasn't. He put his finger on the girl's neck, but couldn't feel anything. There was no re-assuring thump of a pulse. Next he tried her wrist. Again nothing. Finally he put his head on her chest, but could hear no heartbeat.

"What the fuck have you done?" he hissed at Clay still leaning over Dawn's now very much dead body.

"I don't know. I must have given her too much sedative or taken too much blood. Something like that anyway. I didn't mean to, boss, honest." Clay was jabbering, his eyes wild and panicky.

"Fucking hell, this is bloody stupid. This isn't supposed to happen. We're not supposed to harm children. We simply give them a Satanic baptism and then bring them up in our world, keeping them happy and safe from all that Christian mumbo jumbo."

What a fuck up. But what to do now? He'd have to take charge of the situation, issue his instructions and then deal with Clay later on.

"You'll have to get rid of the body, Clay. Maybe you can do that properly without messing it up. Quick, take her away before anyone notices. What the hell am I supposed to say to Brian and Dot who should have taken her home with them?"

Clay didn't reply, just grabbed the girl, slung her over his shoulder like a carcass of meat and pushed his way out of the ruin.

He was absolutely fuming. Why couldn't he find reliable people to join them? Clay had turned out to be a big disappointment to him. It had been Clay who'd let the first girl escape and now he'd killed the second one. He mustn't let the other members of the organisation know; the other chapters that were scattered around the world. If it got out, he'd be seen as nothing more than a bumbling idiot who wasn't even professional enough to get a ritual right.

If Clay couldn't even manage to find and then keep alive a girl for a simple baptism, what might happen when they got on to the bigger rituals, the ones meant to evoke chaos and destruction? The way things stood at the moment, they were managing to evoke chaos and destruction all on their own, without the help of any rituals.

He was beginning to regret his decision to put himself forward as a leader of a new grotto of the Satanic Church when he'd moved into the area. If he'd have known the quality of the membership before he'd opened his big mouth, he wouldn't have bloody bothered. He wasn't sure he could take much more of the pressures of leadership.

It had all seemed so easy back in Birmingham. There the workings of the Satanic Church had run so smoothly, that his assumption was that it would be easy enough for him to run a grotto of his own. Moving to Aldershot had meant that he no longer had the outlet for his sexual fantasies that he'd previously enjoyed through the Church. His wife wasn't into sexual fantasies. In fact she wasn't into sex full stop.

Satan, by one name or another, haunted mankind, tempting him with sweet delights and enlightening him with blinding secrets intended only for gods. He was the one who could be petitioned for powers of retribution and who gave deserved rewards. Instead of creating sins to insure guilty compliance, Satan encouraged indulgence. He was the single deity who could really understand us.

It was a down-to-earth, rational, bedrock philosophy that emphasized the carnal, lustful, natural instincts of man, without imposing guilt for manufactured sins; a philosophy that he fully agreed with. And so it had occurred to him that the best way forward would be to create a new branch of the Satanic Church, with him at the head of it.

But then he found he had to make so many decisions; organise Clay, recruit new members, find suitable premises, order the robes, get copies of the Satanic Bible - the list of things to do seemed endless. Add to that starting a new job and moving house, it wasn't surprising that he was on a short fuse. Buckling under the weight of the latest disaster, he made his way over to Brian and Dot to break the bad news.

Twenty Three

Anderson had been mulling over an idea for some time now and after the success of the past couple of days, had decided that the time was right to approach Superintendent Grimes. He was just about to go upstairs to see him, when the man himself passed Anderson's door, resplendent in full uniform.

"Guv," Derek called, standing up from where he'd been sitting behind his desk. "Have you got a minute?"

Grimes stopped at the door, pulled down his immaculate uniform jacket and looked at his watch. "I've got five minutes actually; I'm just on my way to a presentation so you're lucky to have caught me. What's on your mind?"

"Well, sir, I've had Sgt Major Crane come out with me a couple of times on this mystery child enquiry."

"Oh how is he? Wasn't he the one who had that bad accident?" Grimes said, leaning up against the door frame as there was nowhere to sit in Anderson's office. There rarely was. "Sit down, Derek, do, you look stupid standing there squashed between your desk and the chair."

"Thank you, sir," said Anderson, making himself

comfortable once more. "Yes, he fell out of a lorry, but the thing is, I could really do with him on the team."

"Why?" Grimes looked sceptical and Anderson hoped he'd not made the wrong call. Whilst his boss always said he was approachable and not to hesitate to talk problems through with him, it was well known that Grimes was a career policeman who was going to go far. So good results were because of his leadership and bad ones… Well, those officers who were unfortunate enough to be perceived as having made a mistake were quickly transferred to another department, or even another police station. Anywhere as long as it was out of Grimes' sight.

"Well two reasons really. DS Mulholland, who I usually have working with me, is on paternity leave. And my new DS is being partnered by DC Douglas."

"So? Take someone else from another squad."

"Well, that's my problem, sir. We're all so stretched at the moment working big cases, that it would be bad for moral if I just pulled someone from another team. It'll make them short-handed instead and cause more than a few ructions I can tell you. I wouldn't be the most popular person in the class."

"So what's your solution?" Grimes ran his hand over his already immaculate salt and pepper hair.

"Well, I just wondered..." Derek absentmindedly put his hand up to try to tame his own hair, which didn't work. It never did.

"Yes? Come on, Derek, you've only got 3 of your 5 minutes left." Grimes started to tap his foot.

Derek took a deep breath and said, "Well, I wondered if Crane could partner me? You know how well we've worked together in the past. If you just think of all the cases..."

Grimes interrupted him. "Yes I know all about them and about the legendary Sgt Major Crane. So he's definitely out of the army is he?"

"Yes, retired on medical grounds."

"But isn't that gammy leg of his going to be a problem?" Grimes grimaced, looking as though the last thing he wanted was more problems.

"Not really, sir, we'll be doing interviews and brainstorming and looking at evidence, that sort of thing. Nothing physical."

Grimes stole a glance at his watch. "Well I'm not sure how that would fit in with our own health and safety policies."

"There's also discrimination to consider," said Anderson. "We can't be seen to be discriminating against the disabled."

After a moment Grimes said, "Oh, alright, but on what basis would he join us? He's not part of the police force and I doubt he could join up, he wouldn't pass the physical."

"No, but he could be a special consultant, like we have consultant psychologists, hand writing experts, that sort of thing. My God this place is practically run by civilians. There are civilian evidence gatherers, civilian analysts to decode all the data, forensic staff..." By now Derek was grandstanding.

Grimes put his hand up to stop him. "Alright, I get it, Derek. Well, it's your budget."

"So that's a yes, sir?

"Yes it's a yes," said Grimes standing upright. "If you can persuade Crane, that is," he said as he started to walk away.

"Oh, I don't think I'll have any trouble there, sir," called Derek after him.

Twenty Four

When Ted 'Dunnie' Dunstan woke up at 6 am and looked out of his bedroom window, the world was white. Completely white. The vista was awful enough to chase him back to bed for another hour's kip. However, at 7 am not much had changed, apart from the fact that he couldn't grab yet another hour in bed. He needed to be at the yard for 8 am to let his employees into the compound.

Dawdling as long as he could, he was eventually ready. He'd donned a pair of thermal long johns and vest underneath his blue workman's boiler suit. On top of that went a padded tartan shirt, topped by a gilet, or body warmer to Dunnie and his mates. He had a pair of extra thick socks on inside his steel toe-capped boots and two pairs of gloves on his hands - one with no fingers in and one with. The whole ensemble was topped off by a Russian-type fur hat with ear flaps. A check in the mirror confirmed how he felt; like the Michelin man. Oh how he hated working outdoors in the unpredictable English winter. But working outside had given him a very nice lifestyle, thank you very much, one that his wife particularly enjoyed. Dunnie didn't get to join in so much with the shopping trips, lunches out with her friends and weekends away at health clubs; his role was to make sure he had enough money to pay her credit card bills.

Once outside, his warm breath turning to droplets in the frigid air, he scraped the frost off his windscreen while the engine warmed up. Luckily there was no snow to complicate matters, so it wasn't long before he was on the move, bowling down the road to his compound, a mere 10 minutes' drive away.

Two of the lads were waiting for him when he arrived at the gate and they were puzzling over the lock. Christ Almighty, Dunnie thought, can't they do anything on their own? Now they can't even open up. Leaving the engine of his car running, he clambered out and approached the two men at the gate.

"Open it up for God's sake," he called as he neared them. "What on earth is the matter?"

"The lock's been broken, Dunnie. Look."

"Broken? Has someone broken in?"

Dunnie looked through the gates at his empire. Row upon row of rusting cars were stacked four high, in various stages of being dismantled. Eventually each car would end up crushed into a cube and sold on. But Dunnie was loath to crush a car until he'd managed to get every possible part off it. From where he stood everything looked normal. The crane was parked to one side of the large lot, its hinged arm projecting into the air, looking like some sort of extra-terrestrial being, with the grabber on the end poised to lunch on the empty cars it was guarding. But the colourful rickety piles of abandoned cars were not where the money was. That was in the large wooden building, housing the customer reception and heaps of second-hand parts already taken off the dying vehicles and stored in metal racks. A much tougher place to get into than the front gate.

"Come on," he called to his staff. "Let's go and see what's happened."

It was with some trepidation that he approached the building that looked like nothing more than a tatty shed. But that was only a decoy. The door was secured by an alarm system which could only be opened by the right person with the right thumb print. But all looked well. No one had attempted to prise open the door, not that they'd be able to, what with all the steel rods running through it, which projected into the door frame. There was no alarm clanging in fright and no red lights displayed on the keypad. Dunnie relaxed. All was well.

Unlocking the door he shouted to his men to get on with their day and for someone to drive his car into the compound. He entered the warehouse, turning on lights, booting up computers and turning on the kettle.

He didn't think much about the break-in after that; he was too busy with customers. It was a couple of hours into the morning when he decided to go out into the stacks. He'd had a phone call from a long-standing and highly valued customer who was looking for a particular part of interior trim for an Audi TT. And he just happened to have one. Upon first glance there didn't appear to be a system to the stacks, but they were actually arranged by manufacturer and all the data was held on the computer. So he knew that the car he wanted was in one of the middle stacks towards the far side of the yard.

Whistling as he went, swinging his screwdriver, he was thinking about the accounts. They were due into the tax authorities in a couple of weeks and he reminded himself to ring the accountant when he got back in the office. Finding the TT, he approached it from the rear and was surprised to find that the boot was ajar. It wasn't the biggest boot in the world, a bit snug, but not bad for a convertible sports car. He lifted the lid, intending to slam it down to make sure the lock caught, when he spotted a flash of material push up into the depths of the space. Wondering why there was something in the boot, as they were normally very particular about taking everything out of a car, he put his hand in, expecting to pull out a rag. But he touched something that felt suspiciously like hair. Human hair. He ran his hand down the rags, which were beginning to feel like limbs. And then it moved. Well toppled over to be exact, revealing a young girl, now lying on her back, dressed in a black shift with long blond hair. As he looked at her face, marble white, with open eyes now clouded in death, he backed away and for the first time in his life Dunnie screamed in fear.

Twenty Five

Anderson yet again got the dreaded shout from the doorway, "Got a strange one here for you, guv. Bloke just rang in from the local scrap yard."

"What's wrong, have a few second hand car parts gone missing?"

"No guv, he's not lost anything, he's found something."

"Alright, hit me with it."

"A dead girl. And she's got some marks on her arms."

Anderson stilled for a moment. This was clearly not a time for levity. Surely it couldn't be? Not another poor young girl abducted and tattooed? He glanced at the photo on his desk, showing his own three girls captured on a day out at the beach, fingers of hair whipped by the wind plastered their faces, but couldn't hide their sheer joy at being alive. An involuntary shudder ran through him and his stomach clenched in fear for them. A dead kid - what could be worse? With a sigh he grabbed his suit jacket and called for DS Bullock to come with him, as Crane had a physiotherapy appointment up at the hospital. He could always meet up with Tom at the morgue after he'd been to the scene.

Thirty minutes later Bullock pulled up in front of the scrap yard, let Anderson out and then drove off and parked the car further along up the street, as directed by a traffic policeman. The new DS had been particularly quiet on the drive over, avoiding answering Derek's questions, which were just the usual chit chat about family, and spoken in an effort to divert his mind from the gruesome task ahead. But Bullock had spent most of the drive staring straight ahead, with a death-like grip on the steering wheel. Maybe he was just feeling it too, the tension that was building as they'd driven ever nearer to the crime scene.

Climbing out of the car, Anderson shivered in the cold and pulled his beige mac around him. It was the one that Crane said made him look like Columbo. Unfortunately, much as Anderson liked wearing it, it wasn't built to withstand the morning's cold. Blowing into his cupped hands he called to Bullock who was hesitating and still stood by the car.

"Come on, man, what's the matter with you? Let's get this over with," and with Bullock reluctantly trailing behind, Anderson entered the scrap yard. A uniformed constable directed him to the owner.

"Good morning, I'm DI Anderson and this is DS Bullock from Aldershot police," Derek said. "Perhaps you could tell us what happened, Mr Dunstan."

The large, florid faced man looked up from where he was sitting on the steps of an ambulance, wrapped in one of those heat retaining blanket things, that Anderson always thought looked like tin foil.

"Call me Dunnie, everyone does. I only went to get some interior trim," he said, shaking his head in disbelief. "Never had anything happen like this before."

"I'm sure you haven't, sir. But can we start from the

beginning?"

"Oh, right, well there was a bit of a queer do this morning when we arrived. Someone had broken the padlock on the gates and had obviously gained entry to the yard, but as there was no sign of any intrusion in the warehouse, like, we never thought much of it. Just put it down to kids, like."

Anderson nodded in agreement; the kids in Aldershot, especially from the housing estate nearest to the scrap yard, were a law unto themselves. Feral some would call them. They never did anything really bad, just nicked a bit of lead, shop lifted, ran off with someone's shopping bag in the supermarket; but no matter how many times they were caught and cautioned, it didn't seem to make any difference. Anderson once had a boy who he had sent off with a flea in his ear, turn round and grin at him and flip him the finger from the door of the police station as he was leaving. So much for respect for the police or any sort of authority come to that.

"But it seems it wasn't kids who came into the yard?"

"Nah. Must have been someone dumping the body in one of my cars. Don't know what the world's coming to."

"Could you tell me how you found the girl?"

"She was just pushed into the boot, lying right up against the back of it. Thought it was rags or something that one of the lads had left there by mistake. Such a shock when she rolled over like that and I saw her face." Mr Dunstan's own face began to look like jelly, cheeks wobbling, mouth working, eyes opening and closing. He was clearly in a great deal of distress.

"Sorry, but I have to take him now. He's suffering from shock and we need to get him to hospital." The paramedic spoke in a tone that left no room for dissent, so Anderson nodded his agreement, telling Mr Dunstan that someone would come and see him and take his statement the next day.

"Oh, before you go, are there any CCTV cameras?"

"No, sorry, never felt the need for them. The value is in the warehouse not in the stripped cars."

"Alright, thanks very much. Come on, Bullock, let's go and see the body."

Once again DS Bullock lagged behind and his tentative behaviour was beginning to irritate Anderson. Why couldn't the man walk next to him instead of behind him like some sort of subservient employee? But thoughts of Bullock's strangeness flew out of his head at the sight of the young girl.

She was lying on her back in the small boot of the car, a scrap of a thing, dressed in the same sort of black shift that Hope had been wearing. Some of her blond curls were stuck to her face, but you could still see her eyes. Open. Staring. Opaque. Her stick-like bare arms were covered in various drawings and symbols and there were dark, angry bruises on the back of both hands. Anderson's eyes filled with tears to the point that the scene dissolved before him. But it was no good. He couldn't get the picture of his happy, healthy girls juxtaposed with the poor dead child in the boot, out of his head. Behind him he could hear DS Bullock throwing up.

Twenty Six

Anderson sent Bullock back to the police station in a traffic car, glad to be rid of the man who seemed to irk him no matter what he did, and made his solitary way to Frimley Park Hospital, managing to catch Crane as he emerged from the Rehabilitation Suite.

Crane said, "That doesn't look good."

"What?"

"Your face. I've got pain as an excuse for my grimaces, what's yours?"

"I need a coffee first."

Crane said, "Sounds good to me, come on," and led the way to the cafeteria on the ground floor.

Once sat at an empty table Crane shook a sachet of sugar and emptying it into his cup said, "This coffee's abysmal, but at least it's hot and wet. So, what's happened?"

Looking at his friend, with a broken body, yet still razor sharp mind, albeit dulled by pain medication, Anderson was suddenly very glad Crane was there. His friend and confidant for years now, Derek had been desperate not to lose his company and expertise.

"We found another girl. Another Hope."

"Hell's teeth. Where is she? When can we see her?"

"In the morgue and now."

Crane slowly put his coffee cup back on the saucer with just the smallest of tremors in his hand. Once it was safely back on the table he said, "You mean this one's dead?"

Anderson nodded.

"Jesus, Derek, you don't pull any punches do you?"

"Sorry. I'm not feeling very subtle at the moment."

"No, I don't suppose you are. Come on, tell me."

Anderson started his story, keeping his eyes on the table, rather than on his friend, for if he saw Crane having an emotional reaction to the death of a child, he wouldn't be able to hold it together.

At the end of his retelling, Crane coughed, as though clearing his throat of emotion and said, "What can I do to help?"

"Join the team."

"Sorry?"

"Is there something wrong with your ears? I'm asking you to formally join the investigating team, then we can go down to the morgue and you can see the body."

"Is this on the level?"

"Of course, I've got approval to employ you as a civilian consultant." Anderson looked straight into his friend's eyes and so as not to give Crane any chance of dalliance said, "So are you in? I need to know now, so we can get on with it."

Crane looked out at the weeping willow for a moment; the tree that Anderson felt was now weeping for two children. Then he turned and grinned. "I've no idea how you managed to swing that, but you bet I'm in. If you can put up with me dressed in my loose comfortable clothing as required by my physiotherapist,"

Crane indicated his track suit, tee shirt and trainers, "Then come on, let's get out of here," and he grabbed his stick.

***

"Listen up, people," Anderson called as he and Crane entered the Incident Room. "Before we get started, most of you know Sgt Major Crane here, well this is just to confirm that he is now officially part of the team, so work with him, discuss the case with him and generally do your best to make him welcome."

All eyes turned towards Crane who rather self-consciously waved his stick in greeting.

"Must we, guv?" quipped one joker to titters and smiles from the team.

"Yes, otherwise he'll inflict on you his own brand of army punishment. You could find yourselves doing 50 press ups right here on the office floor if you're not careful. So, does anyone else have any questions about Crane? No? I thought not. Right, on to matters in hand."

Anderson and Crane discussed with the team the death of the unknown girl and Anderson showed photographs of the markings on her arm. He allocated someone the task of comparing and contrasting those on the dead girl, with those on Hope.

As yet they had no cause of death, nor time of death, as they were awaiting the results of the post mortem that would take place that afternoon.

"How are forensics doing?" he asked DC Douglas.

"Still there at the scrap yard, guv. They think it will take the rest of the day to process the scene."

"Alright, make sure they put this one at the very top of their list, will you? And ask them to let us have information as and when they get it. I don't want them to wait to file a complete report, I'm happy to have the results drip fed."

"Yes, guv."

Anderson carried on allocating tasks, and then he got to DS Bullock.

"Check missing persons again will you, Bullock?"

"If you say so, but nothing local came up last time, boss."

Anderson wasn't sure he'd heard right. Not only had Bullock just questioned his order in front of the whole team, which was bad enough in itself, but it was specifically what he'd just said. Anger flared within him and as a result he hissed his reply, "Local? You mean to tell me you only did a local search for missing children?"

Anderson had always thought Bullock a bit strange, but it never occurred to him that as a detective sergeant he would be bloody thick to boot.

"Well yes, boss, the way I saw it was - how would a young girl get lost in this area unless she lived here?"

Anderson rarely belittled his staff in public, but by God this time it was well deserved.

"You fucking idiot. Didn't you think that the girl could have been abducted from anywhere in the country and brought here? Now do a proper UK-wide missing persons search on both girls before I have your balls for breakfast."

"Yes, guv," said Bullock, his fair skin flaming pink, clashing with his ginger hair.

Twenty Seven

Over supper Crane broke the good news to Tina. Or at least it was good news as far as he was concerned. He hoped Tina would agree with his decision to join the team. He could already feel the benefits of doing something useful, being accepted as an investigator once again and having a reason to get up in the morning.

"So, what do you think? I'm sorry I didn't talk to you first, but Derek rather put me on the spot. I needed to agree there and then, so I could view the body in the morgue."

Crane ignored his food and concentrated on Tina's reaction.

"Please, Tom! Do you have to talk about dead bodies," Tina grimaced. "I'm eating," she indicated the fish and chips on her plate.

"Oh, right. Sorry." Crane had never had a problem talking about a dead body over food, but he guessed it took all sorts. Tina was clearly talking from a civilian point of view.

"What about the practical stuff? Are they paying you? What are the hours? Is it full-time, or part-time?"

"Yes, apparently they are paying me, but I don't really

need the money, not any more, not with you working and the medical discharge pension. And this isn't about the money anyway."

"I never thought you'd be doing it for the money, Tom, what do you think of me? I hoped you'd be doing it for the chance to keep making a difference." Tina grabbed her glass of wine and took a sip. It seemed to help keep her emotions under control as she then said calmly, "But there's still your recovery to take into account."

"What do you mean?"

"Oh, come on, Tom," Tina pushed her plate away. "You know exactly what I mean. You've still got physiotherapy to go to. There's a limit as to what you can do physically and if you push yourself too hard, will you be able to cope with the pain?"

"I've thought about that," Crane tried hard to keep the sullen tone of his voice, but didn't really manage it. Why was Tina making this supposedly happy event into something very different?

Tina looked askance, clearly not believing him.

"I did, honestly," Crane crossed his fingers behind his back. "But I decided that a mystery child and a dead girl were more important than any additional discomfort I may experience as a result of assisting in the investigation."

Tina laughed. "Well that was a good army speak reply if ever I heard one."

Crane grinned glad he'd broken her bad mood. "You know what I mean," he said, finishing the last of his fish.

"This case has really got under your skin hasn't it," Tina grabbed Crane's hand where it lay on the table.

He squeezed hers in return. "Yes, love it has. It's got to Derek as well. He's got three girls…" Crane tailed off, unable to finish his sentence, fighting with his own emotions, thinking back to when he'd found a dead baby on the steps of the Garrison Church and then had been unable to save another one.

Tina filled the silence. "You two work so well together, and if anyone can solve this case, I know you can."

"But I wonder what happens at the end of the case... Or if we run into a brick wall and they close down the team...What will I do then?" Crane vocalised the doubts he had about the arrangement.

"I think you should stop worrying about that and concentrate on the present."

"Yes, I suppose I've had a lot of experience doing that recently, what with the accident and my recovery and all."

Hearing Daniel crying through the baby monitor, Tina stood up, "Go for it, Tom. Daniel and I will be fine and I'll always be here to give you any support you need. Go and do what do best," she said, kissing him and then running up the stairs to check on their son.

Crane wiped away his sudden tears. What the hell was wrong with him? Since the accident he seemed to be wearing his heart on his proverbial sleeve. Well that would have to stop. Right now. He pushed himself up from the table and started clearing up while he waited for Tina to come back downstairs.

Twenty Eight

Crane and Anderson were in the DI's office going over the case before the morning briefing, when the phone interrupted them.

"Dr McAllister here," the psychiatrist said, "I've got an update for you." Then as if realising she'd been rather too brusque said, "Sorry, if you've got a minute that is."

Anderson smiled, even though the Doctor couldn't see him. "No worries. I'm going to put you on speaker, as I've Crane with me." He mouthed who it was to Crane before pressing the speaker button on his handset.

"Right, Doc, what do you have for us?"

"I've just left Hope and I think you'll be very interested in her latest picture. She's drawn an ice cream van and next to it…"

"Is a picture of her eating an ice cream?" Anderson guessed.

"Exactly, DI Anderson."

"Can you take a picture of it on your phone and send it to us straight away?" Crane asked.

"Of course, I'll send it over via WhatsApp, and I'll get the original over to you as soon as I can. I hope this information helps?"

"Oh, most definitely," agreed Anderson. "It's very much in-line with our thinking. How is Hope?"

"Alright. Fairly stable at the moment."

"Did it upset her, drawing the picture?"

"No, Crane, she seemed quite calm and in fact seemed to view drawing the picture with a sense of achievement, as if she knew that her memory would eventually be able to help find out who did the awful thing to her."

"That's excellent work, thanks, Doc, I look forward to seeing the picture," and Anderson ended the call. "Well that's a turn up for the books," he said to Crane.

"It's confirmation of what you thought, or rather DC Douglas thought."

Anderson nodded and couldn't help grinning. "This is the best lead we've had so far on the case. Come on, let's go and brief the team."

Anderson pushed out of his chair and went out of the door with Crane following on behind, and called the team together. Once everyone was looking up and had finished their phone calls, or their work on the computers, he told them about the new picture Hope had drawn and throwing his phone to Douglas, told him to distribute the photograph to the rest of the team.

"So, the question is, did we get anywhere with the ice cream van angle? Weren't you doing that DS Bullock?"

"No, sir, I was," blurted DC Douglas.

"Why? I'm sure I asked DS Bullock to look into it."

"Um, because DS Bullock asked me to? Um, was that alright?" Douglas was very flustered, looking from Anderson to Bullock and back again and then at Crane for good measure.

"Yes, that's fine." Anderson didn't see any point in shouting at Douglas. Bullock was really the one he needed to shout at. Again.

"So, as I was asking, did you get anywhere with the ice cream van angle?"

Anderson was having trouble reigning in his temper, but it wasn't directed at DC Douglas, but at DS Bullock. The new DS was definitely getting on his nerves and he needed to get a handle on his anger. He looked over at Bullock who held Anderson's gaze. But then Bullock's eyes went strangely blank, as though he were deliberately pulling the shutters down. Anderson couldn't gauge Bullock's feelings, as the man retreated to some private place inside his head.

Derek had never seen that happen on the face of a policeman. But he had definitely been subject to that look before. He'd seen it in the eyes of murderers and psychopaths. The thought made Anderson shudder and it was with a great mental effort that he turned his attention back to DC Douglas, trying to tell himself that he was over-reacting in his anger and paranoia.

"There's nothing local, guv," said Douglas. "No one has any vans missing. All the businesses seem legit and I can't find any previous on any of their employees. So I left that and went onto other things."

Local. Anderson had heard that before. From DS Bullock.

"And who said you should keep the search to local firms?" Anderson kept his voice measured, fighting with his natural instinct to shout.

"Um, well, DS Bullock, of course." Douglas seemed to be physically shrinking, backing into his chair as if to get away from the trouble that he was potentially in.

"Well, I'm telling you to expand the search. Please."

"Where to, guv?" Douglas' voice waivered.

"Jesus Christ," Anderson eventually exploded with

the fury that had been building throughout the exchange. "Do I have to hold your hands on this?" he shouted. "Start with the whole of the South of England and then work your way up the Country."

"But that's going to take ages," Douglas said in a small voice.

"Do I look like I care how long it takes, Douglas? Now bloody well get on with it." He paused to take a breath and then added, "And DS Bullock?"

"Yes, guv?"

"I'll be speaking to you later, in my office. In the meantime, I suggest you also get on with doing your job properly and stop trying to cut corners. Do I make myself clear?"

"Yes, guv," Bullock said as everyone swivelled to look at him, their attention switching from poor DC Douglas to him.

"And that goes for all of you!" Anderson shouted as a finale, before turning on his heel and stalking back to his office.

Once they were safely ensconced in Anderson's office, Crane shut the door and wanted to know why Anderson was so angry. "I've never seen you shout at your team like that before, Derek. Are you learning from me? You sounded pretty much like a Sgt Major out there."

"This bloody case is getting to me, Crane," Anderson confessed as he relaxed somewhat. It's my girls, see..." Anderson shook his head, then took a deep breath and swallowed.

"Sorry, Derek, I should have thought. How old are they now?"

"9, 12 and 15. It could have been any one of them that turned up dead, but especially the youngest. How can I keep them safe, Crane? How can I stop any more girls going missing or getting killed? I don't have a bloody clue who's doing this or why? It's eating me up, I know. But I have to keep going. I have to find out who's behind this."

"We will, Derek. You don't have to shoulder the responsibility all on your own, you know. We're in this together. And last time I checked we were a bloody good team. Or at least you always told me we were."

Anderson wanted to tell his friend how much his words meant to him and how glad he was that they were able to work together once again. But the words wouldn't come out. They seemed stuck in his throat. But he guessed it didn't matter. He didn't need to explain anything to Crane. They knew each other too well. But DS Bullock was altogether another matter. He didn't know him at all.

"What's our next move?" Crane asked.

"A closer look at DS Bullock, would be a very good place to start."

Twenty Nine

Bullock was fuming after another dressing down in public. Who the hell did Anderson think he was? If this was what it was like working down South, then he wished he'd stayed in the Midlands. At least there he'd known the bosses, knew how they thought, what made them tick. But here, well he was at a loss. Still reeling from the shock and embarrassment he got up from his desk and blundered to the toilets, where he washed his face with cold water in an attempt to calm down. As he looked at his reflection in the mirror he couldn't see any outward reason for Anderson's distrust of him. He looked normal. Ordinary. Okay, so he had ginger hair and pale freckled skin, but hey if Ed Sheenan could get away with it...

The fact of the matter was that he'd never been spoken to like that before. No one would have done that in his previous division. He had made a carefully considered decision about where to search for the missing children and which ice cream businesses to investigate. It was just that his decisions didn't gel with Anderson's decisions. But only Bullock knew why. He had been hoping that stupid DC Douglas would take all the blame if his orders ever came to light, but the rat Douglas had told Anderson that it was Bullock who had controlled what Douglas did and didn't do, putting him right in the headlights. It just proved that it didn't do to rely on subordinates.

Anyway, he hadn't yet recovered from the body of the girl being found and so quickly too. Fucking Clay. He'd told Clay to hide her somewhere where she wouldn't be found for a long, long time and look what had happened - she'd been found the very next day. Driving Anderson to the scrap yard had been pure agony. He'd had trouble, firstly trying to keep his temper with Clay and secondly with the building horror at what he would find at the crime scene. And how he'd react to it, especially under the scrutiny of Anderson. It was all Clay's fault, of course. He'd let the first girl escape and had killed the second by giving her too much tranquiliser. Fancy giving her ketamine. She was half the bloody size of a horse.

But he shouldn't have thrown up at the scene. That really had been a sign of weakness. It was just that everything seemed to build up inside of him and he couldn't stop it all blowing out, a bit like a geyser. His body showed the physical sign of the inner turmoil he was going through. It had made him look like an amateur, like someone who hadn't seen a dead body before. He would be the laughing stock of the incident room if it got out.

He fervently wished he was still up in the Midlands.

Which led him to decide that all of this, if he was honest, was his wife Enid's fault. Yes, that was it. It was her. All her. He had only joined the Satanists because she was so bloody ugly; with her straight black hair that looked like a helmet on her head and her dowdy clothes and flat shoes. Let's face it, who wouldn't look elsewhere for a bit of sexual excitement? She took 'lying back and thinking of England' to a whole new level. Sometimes, earlier on in their marriage when they were still having sex, he'd been convinced that he'd killed her as she would just lie there; pale faced, not moving and hardly breathing.

They'd had to move down to Aldershot for her, the stupid bitch, as she wanted to be closer to her elderly parents, who were beginning to show signs of old age. The two old codgers kept coming down with lots of different illnesses and were always at the doctor's surgery or the hospital for this, that, or the other. To be honest he didn't really know what was wrong with them exactly, as he didn't listen to her when she tried to tell him. He switched off and thought about something else, or read the paper, or watched the television while she droned on and on and on. She seemed happy as long as he put in the odd, 'um', 'yeah', and 'oh dear'. And don't even get him started on their memory loss. It was a wonder they could remember their own names!

She seemed to be at their house morning, noon and night. He supposed that at least it meant he could work late and start early without her moaning. And it also meant that he could go out and organise the chapter of the Satanic Church on his free evenings. She went to bed so early from exhaustion, that it meant he was free to come and go and he pleased. Which brought him back to the thorny subject of Clay. Just wait till he got his hands on him. Hands that would more than likely end up around his neck.

Thirty

To give his hip a rest, Crane was sitting at a desk with a computer in the incident room. He watched as Bullock walked back in. His face was damp from what at first Crane thought was sweat, but as the man's shirt cuffs were also damp, he realised Bullock had more than likely been washing his face. Crane wasn't sure about the man either, but he wondered if Anderson's reaction to Bullock's faux pas had been a bit over the top. For some reason Bullock seemed to push Anderson's buttons, but that didn't mean that Bullock was guilty of anything. The last time he looked, being a bit of a tit wasn't against the law.

Crane liked it in the incident room. There was lots of buzz, coffee and Anderson's stash of sweet cakes and biscuits was only a stone's throw away. But then again he needed to keep off them otherwise he'll start getting fat. He'd lost a lot of weight after his accident and needed to bulk up, but he mustn't go overboard. Carrying too much weight would exacerbate his pain, because of the pressure it would put on his injuries and joints. But at the moment his suits hung on him and he knew he looked gaunt and drained, as though he wasn't very well, which of course was right on the money. But this new job, working with Anderson, would be good for him. He could feel it, the old excitement fizzing up inside him. There was nothing better than doing something that you were good at and that made a difference. His forte was putting away those who were happy to break the law, but were seriously pissed off once they got caught.

A twinge in his hip brought him back to reality. Tina was right, he mustn't overdo it. But then when she talked like that, he also sometimes wondered if he would be able to keep up with Anderson with his physical disability. His greatest fear being that the bloody gammy leg would let him down just at the wrong time. The last thing he wanted was to stare failure in the face. Making a success of this job was very important to him, to say the least.

Which reminded him that it was about time he got on with it. He'd been looking up the various symbols that they'd found on both girls. Most were different, but there was one that both girls had, at the top of each arm. It was the old alchemist sign for sulphur. But what was more worrying was the fact that it was often associated with Satanism. Crane clicked on a link in the search engine and read on...

The alchemical element sulphur (Brimstone). The symbol of sulphur was often used as an identifying symbol by Satanists, due to sulphur's historical association with the Devil. This glyph was often referred to as the "pontifical cross of Satan" by Christian tract writers, due to its adoption as an emblem of Satanism by Anton LaVey in the 1960s. The emblem had no history as a symbol of Satanism outside of LaVey's usage, and the attribution was most likely a product of anti-Catholic sentiment, as it was often compared in this context to the Catholic Pontifical Cross.

Brimstone eh? Somewhere in the depths of his memory was a snippet: fire and brimstone. He thought that was normally associated with witches. But it seemed as though there could be a connection with Satanism. Who was this Anton LaVey? It was certainly not a name he'd ever come across before. Crane clicked on another link.

LaVeyan Satanism was a philosophy and new religious movement founded in 1966 by American author and occultist Anton LaVey. The religion's doctrines and practices were codified in The Satanic Bible and overseen by the Church of Satan.

Satanism involved the practice of magic, which encompassed two distinct forms; greater and lesser magic. Greater magic was a form of ritual practice and was meant as psycho-dramatic catharsis to focus one's emotional energy for a specific purpose. These rites were based on three major psycho-emotive themes, including compassion (love), destruction (hate), and sex (lust). Lesser magic was the practice of manipulation by means of applied psychology and glamour (or 'wile and guile') to bend an individual or situation to one's will. LaVey wrote extensively on the subject of ritual in his works, The Satanic Bible and The Satanic Rituals, and on lesser magic in The Satanic Witch.

A quick check on Amazon showed that these books were readily available to purchase, including in eBook format. What the fuck? Crane was about to shout for Anderson, when he realised he was no longer a Sgt Major, sat in his office, with subordinates at his beck and call. No longer the man who spearheaded an investigation and who decided which way the inquiry went.

His fists instinctively clenched and his teeth ground together. It just wasn't bloody fair, that was the crux of the matter. He'd had such a good life before the accident. For that's what the army had been to him. His life. It was often said that being in the army came before family. It was true enough for the good soldiers, the ones who took pride in their regiments, those who fully embraced what the army stood for; as Crane had done. It was hard not to think that although he'd never let the army down, the army had let him down. They shouldn't have made the unilateral decision that Crane had to leave. Some days he felt like a discarded toy. Some days he felt like throwing a childish tantrum and shouting, 'It's not fair!' at anyone who would listen.

"You alright, guv?" DC Douglas' voice floated over to him. "Only you're going a funny colour. Is the hip playing up? Is there anything I can do to help?"

The simple kindness in the offer of help and the concern in Douglas' voice cut through Crane's malevolent introspection, causing the sides of his mouth to tug upwards into the semblance of a smile. Making a conscious decision to get over himself, and to swallow down the anger that always blossomed when faced with his change of circumstances and current limitations, he said, "Just a bit, but I'll be alright. Thanks, though."

Crane printed off the pages he'd been reading and clumped his way to Anderson's office. He might not be in charge, but he was part of the team and had Anderson's ear, and that would do for now.

Thirty One

When Crane arrived with his papers, Anderson was reading the post-mortem report on the dead girl.

"Oh, Crane, glad you're here. Sit down and listen to this."

Crane complied, his papers still clutched in his hand.

"Right, there are startling similarities between Hope and the dead girl. The post-mortem has revealed extensive blood loss with draining points on the back of both hands."

Crane felt a bit faint at that revelation and was glad he was sitting down. "Is there nowhere else the blood loss could have come from?"

Anderson flicked through the pages. "No, no other injuries were found. So the pathologist had no option but to believe that the blood loss was through the hands."

"Any sexual abuse?"

"No, nothing. No injuries, tearing or bruising and she was still a virgin."

"Thank God for small mercies," Crane said. "Has he got an age for her?"

"Yes, between 11 and 12 years old."

Crane dwelt on that for a moment. "So how did they,

whoever they are, make her pliable?"

"She died from an overdose of tranquiliser. Ketamine. Who the hell would do that? And why would they do it?"

Crane looked down at the papers still scrunched up in his hand. "I might have an idea about that. Here."

After a few minutes of silent reading Anderson looked up and said, "You can't be serious?"

"Deadly, if you'll excuse the pun. Look, both these girls were being used for some sort of ritual and it's clear that the marks drawn on their arms had some sort of religious connotations. You can't disagree with the evidence, Derek."

"No, you're right there. But I was leaning towards it being some sort of Druid activity, or a strange gathering of like-minded people. Not this," he handed Crane's papers back.

"Sorry, but I think you're wrong." Crane was determined to make his case and leaned forward, elbows on his knees. "It seems to me something more sinister than just a casual gathering. You don't drain the blood of young virgins for nothing. In fact you don't drain their blood for any sane reason. I think you just don't want to face the fact that something evil could be behind all of this."

"No, you're right I don't. After that awful article by Diane Chambers, I've deliberately stayed away from all of that hocus pocus. Dear God, can you imagine how the local community would react to the idea that there really is some sort of Devil worship being practised in their midst? It was bad enough when Diane's article was published and so I can't give any credence to such theories."

"I know - there would be mass hysteria. But we can't

ignore it, Derek and it might even help us find the sick bastards that have done this."

"No, sorry, Crane, I can't agree with you. Not this time."

"Fair enough I'll keep my mouth shut. But only if you let me work that angle."

"I just said…"

"I know what you just said. That's why I'm saying that only I will look at the idea that Devil worship could be behind this. I'll even do it on my own time at home, if it makes you feel any better."

"Jesus, Crane. Oh alright. But not a word of this to anyone else. No one in the team and not even Tina."

"Thanks, Derek," said Crane and made his awkward way out of the door.

Closing the door of Derek's office behind him, a relieved Crane turned to return to his work station. He'd got what he wanted. Long ago he'd realised that the best way to get what you wanted out of superior officers was to ask for something inflated. Something that would never be approved. Then subsequently, he would ask for what he had wanted all along, which then appeared to be a reasonable request in the light of his outlandish demand. It worked every time and Derek had fallen for the ploy as well. With more than a modicum of satisfaction Crane hobbled his way back to his desk. But someone was there. Looking at his computer. And from the looks of it, checking Crane's browsing history.

Thirty Two

He would have to be careful. Anderson was beginning to give him looks. Those side-ways ones that meant Anderson couldn't quite make his mind up about him, wasn't sure about the new boy. Even though he'd been at Aldershot for over three months now, it didn't seem enough to allay Anderson's doubts. Bullock had thought he'd managed to integrate himself into the team rather well, but now he wasn't so sure. This case was spooking everybody and as a result Anderson was turning on the person he knew the least. It was beginning to give him headaches.

Bullock's head was down, and he was pretending to be absorbed in his work. But really he was somewhere else. Somewhere in his head. His attention wasn't on the office, the file in front of him, or the computer screen by his elbow. He was thinking hard about Clay and what he was going to do about him. Or do to him. Yes, do to him sounded better. The bloody idiot had put the new Chapter of the Satanic Church at risk. He'd had to contact his other partners in… in what? What was the best way of describing those like-minded people who just enjoyed getting together for a bit of fun? No, fun wasn't the right word. Those who were looking for something else, a something that would bring a bit of excitement into their humdrum lives. Looking for something to interest them, absorb them and allow the release of their pent up feelings and frustrations at their boring and worthless lives. So, partners in crime, which was the word he was first thinking of, wasn't quite right. There shouldn't have been any crime involved in it anywhere. If the first girl hadn't escaped, then there would never have been a second who had died. The whole operation was in danger of tumbling down like a house of cards. He'd have to get in touch with them all, get them to lie low for a while, tell them he'd be in touch again when it was safe to continue.

"Are you alright, guv?"

DC Douglas' voice broke through his reverie and Bullock realised that he'd been gripping the cheap ballpoint pen in his hand so hard that it had snapped.

"What? Yes, fine, why wouldn't I be?" he said sweeping the broken bits of plastic into the bin.

"No reason, you just seemed, um, elsewhere."

"I'm doing my job, Douglas, by concentrating on the case, which is more than you seem to be doing."

"Sorry, guv, I'll get back to it then."

"What a good idea," said Bullock, the drip of sarcasm clear in his voice, causing Douglas to scurry back to his desk.

He supposed he'd better get back to it too. There was no point in dwelling on the past. He'd have to look towards the future. Surely when all this had died down, he could start the Chapter meetings again. As long as no one found the farm house. Oh God, he'd never thought of that. Waves of fear ran up and down his spine, chilling him and causing a tremor to run through his body.

"Got anything yet, Bullock?"

The sound of Crane's voice made him start.

"Sorry?" he mumbled.

"The missing persons search, have you found anyone that fits the description of our girl yet?"

Bullock clenched his teeth and took a deep breath. He hated Crane as much as he hated Anderson. Those two were thick as thieves, more so since Crane had been officially recognised as part of the team. He couldn't see the attraction in the ex-army detective himself. Crane came across as cold, distant, authoritative and because of that he seemed to behave as though he were better than everyone else on the team. God, he wished he were still in Birmingham.

"No, not yet, Crane, it's a long job. And if you don't leave me alone I won't get through it at all will I?"

Bullock was hoping his reply would put Crane in his place, but it seemed not. Crane simply stood there with a self-satisfied smile on his face, before turning and limping away. Bastard.

Bullock guessed it was in his best interests to get on with the job and turned his attention back to the computer. The search that he'd done of missing girls, age range 5-12, white, blond hair, had turned up a surprising number of them. But then, he guessed it would, as he was searching all of the UK. He flicked through more records, Brighton, Barnstable, Birmingham. Shit! Birmingham. Staring out at him from his computer screen was her – the dead girl - his dead girl. He looked around the office, surreptitiously, head still down, eyes up as he scanned the room. No one seemed to be paying him any attention; Douglas was on the phone, Anderson in his office, Crane typing something on his keyboard and the rest of the team were beavering away as well. He could feel the sweat breaking through on his face; each tiny drop bursting like spots that were popping and spreading puss all over his skin. His hand shook as he grabbed his mouse. Just two clicks were all it would take to eliminate the record entirely. Holding his breath, he made the first click. A little box came up. *Delete record - yes or no?* Unable to resist, he glanced around the room once more, then clicked 'Yes'. It was done. He was safe.

"Douglas!" he shouted and the young man came scurrying over from the photocopying machine.

"Yes, guv?"

"Are those the ice cream company details you've got there?"

"Um, yes they are."

"Good, give them to me and we'll swap jobs. I'll do the ice cream vans and you can take over the missing persons."

"Why?"

"Because I bloody said so!" Bullock realised he was shouting. "It'll keep us fresh, save brain fog. Alright?"

"Of course, guv. Whatever you say. You're the boss."

"Exactly, I am, now get on with it. I've done up to the Midlands, so you can go further up the country."

Thank God for subordinates, thought Bullock. Now no one would know that a record had been deleted and more importantly wouldn't know who had done it. One more problem solved. But as he realised how close he'd come to being found out, his stomach cramped and his bowels churned.

Thirty Three

"Yes!"

The shout rang out around the incident room and everyone stopped what they were doing and looked at DC Douglas as though he were some sort of idiot. Douglas' face burned as Anderson walked out from his office to find out what was going on.

He said, "I take it there's been a development?"

"Yes, sorry, boss, but I think I've found her," Douglas said, rising from his seat and hopping from one foot to another, as though he was a marionette, and someone was jerking his strings.

"Found who?" said Crane as he joined Anderson.

"Hope. I've found her missing person's record. She was reported missing in Birmingham about three weeks ago. Bloody hell! I did it!"

Anderson closed his eyes and muttered a prayer of thanks. At last, a major breakthrough in the case. He looked at Crane who was swaying, holding onto his stick so tightly his fingers were white.

"Here," he pulled up a chair. "Sit before you fall down."

Crane sank into a chair, put his stick between his legs

and leant on it.

"Douglas," prompted Anderson, "Could you tell us a bit more?"

"Oh, shit, right, sorry. Her name is Bethany Franks from Birmingham... um... sorry, just a minute," Douglas sat down and pulled his chair closer to the screen. "She's 10 years old, nearly 11 actually, lives at home with her parents and two sisters and, oh my God listen to this, she was last seen a couple of streets away from her home and a witness remembers hearing the tune of an ice cream van in the vicinity."

If it had been an office in the United States, Douglas might have expected a round of applause, cheers, hand shaking and back slapping. But as it was Aldershot, England, the reaction was far more understated, muted even. Crane grinned, Anderson nodded and the rest of the team frankly just looked relieved. At last a lead they could work and more importantly, they knew who Hope was and could re-unite her with her parents. It was a major achievement, the information found by DC Douglas, but born from a bollocking from Anderson.

"Good work, Douglas," said Anderson, all business. "Now print the record off, please and give copies to everyone. I'll get in touch with the local Birmingham nick and bring them up to date. They'll send someone round to her parents, who will no doubt be here in a few hours. Crane and I will handle that side of things, go to the hospital meet her parents and liaise with the medical staff. DS Bullock can you get a copy of the full file emailed over for us? Go through the witness statements and see if you can find anything that correlates with what we already know from this end. Douglas, I want you to concentrate on the details of the ice cream van, canvass businesses in the area and get photographs from them.

We need to identify that bloody van."

"Yes, guv," said Douglas, still pink around the ears from his triumph, "I'll get on it straight away."

Anderson and Crane went back to the DI's office where Anderson couldn't resist a high five with his friend. But that was the extent of their celebration. It was time to get down to work, but then DC Douglas coming into the office and handing him a copy of the computer record, sparked a memory.

Anderson said, "Douglas, if I remember rightly, you were working on the ice cream van angle weren't you and DS Bullock on the missing persons?"

"Well, um, yes, guv, that was what was initially going on."

"Initially?"

Douglas nodded.

"So what changed? How come you're now working on the missing persons?"

"Oh, DS Bullock asked me to, sir. He said a swop of jobs would keep us on our toes, you know a change is a good as a rest and all that." Douglas seemed to realise Anderson was glaring at him, not smiling and stammered, "W, w, was that okay, sir? He sort of, well intimated that it was your idea, sir. And I guess it doesn't matter, not really, because I found her didn't I?"

Anderson didn't have the heart to berate DC Douglas. It wasn't the young man's fault as he was only taking orders from a superior officer.

"No, that's fine, Douglas, thanks for the information, oh and well done again lad."

Anderson was rewarded with a beaming smile.

Crane said, "Bullock again."

"Yes. Bullock again. What the bloody hell is going on with that man? I'll have to get to the bottom of it. But not now. Now we've got work to do," and Anderson reached for the phone.

Thirty Four

It was time. They had arrived. Anderson looked at Crane and nodded, this wasn't going to be one of the easiest interviews they'd ever done. Wordlessly Anderson left the room. Crane followed him and then watched from the door as Anderson said, "Mr and Mrs Franks, I'm very glad to meet you, I'm DI Anderson of the Aldershot Police."

"Where's our daughter?"

"When can we see Bethany?"

Mr and Mrs Franks spoke at the same time and were looking anxiously around as they stood at the entrance to the ward where Bethany was, barely able to keep still, craning their necks for their first glimpse of their daughter.

"Let's just have a chat for a minute, shall we? My colleague Sgt Major Crane and I would like you to come into the family room first."

"What? Really? Why can't I see my daughter now? Right away?" Mrs Franks was becoming strident in her repeated requests to see Bethany as she was herded away from the ward and Crane couldn't blame her, but Anderson insisted that he needed to prepare them first.

"Please sit down," Anderson said.

"What? Why? Is there something wrong with her?"

"No, Mrs Franks, there's nothing wrong as such, but Bethany has been severely traumatised by her ordeal."

Crane kept out of the conversation, preferring to watch the parents. Mr Franks wasn't saying much, but he put his hand over his wife's. Was it a sign of solidarity, of comfort, or did he want her to shut up? Either way it worked, as she fell silent and looked at him, smiling at his gesture. A sign of comfort then. They both looked rather bedraggled. Mr Franks had casual clothes on underneath his overcoat and his hair looked as though he'd been running his hands through it all the way from Birmingham, which to be fair he probably had. Mrs Frank's face was devoid of any make-up and her eyes were red rimmed. Crane hoped that at last they were tears of joy, not of sadness. She pulled together the edges of her short coat and shivered slightly despite the warmth of the room.

"I don't know what Birmingham have told you, but…"

"Nothing really," Mr Franks butted in. "Just that you'd found her alive and well and that she was in hospital being treated for shock. Do you know what happened to her? Where has she been? Who had taken her?"

"That's what I'm trying to explain to you," Anderson was calm and patient despite the questions being fired at him. "Your daughter was last seen a few streets from her home, is that correct?"

"Yes, she heard the ice cream van and wanted an ice cream. I didn't think much about it at the time," said Mrs Franks. "I just gave her a quid to buy one as I was busy in the kitchen and she said she'd be right back."

"But she didn't come back," said Mr Franks. "We waited and waited, but in the end we had to call the police and report her missing."

"We've been in a living hell since then," Mrs Franks finished for her husband.

Indeed they both looked gaunt and had that hollow-eyed look that frightened parents had as they were traipsed across the TV screens by concerned police forces, their anguish lapped up by the media. Crane didn't know for sure, but it was a safe bet that they had been on the local Birmingham television news programmes.

"I'm sure you have, the wait must have been awful. Well, as strange as it may seem, Hope, sorry, I mean Bethany…"

"Why aren't you calling her Bethany? That's her name. Not Hope. Where did you get Hope from?"

Crane could see his friend struggling with that question. Anderson made several attempts to speak, opening and then closing his mouth again. In the end Crane squared his shoulders as if bracing himself for the shock and outrage he was expecting from Mr and Mrs Franks and spoke. "Your daughter won't speak. As we didn't know her name, we wanted to call her something more personal than Jane Doe." Mrs Franks flinched at that reference to unidentified females. "So as we always hoped we could find out what happened to her, we referred to her as Hope."

"What? She won't speak?"

"Why not? Is her throat damaged?"

"No, Mrs Franks, there's nothing wrong with her voice. The doctors think she's become a selective mute, as she is still traumatised from her abduction."

Mr Franks said, "Will she remember us?"

Mrs Franks said, "Do you think she knows her own name?"

"Yes and yes. But helping children who have undergone trauma is not an exact science. Bethany," Anderson said her name slowly as if he were making sure he didn't get it wrong again, "has been working with a Child Psychologist, Dr McAllister. She seems well physically and is communicating with the doctor through drawing therapy."

As Mrs Franks broke down, sobbing into a handkerchief she had dragged from her coat pocket, Mr Franks said, "What on earth happened to her?"

"At the moment, we're not sure. She was abducted and brought to this area, but managed to escape somehow, but we don't know from where, as she was found wandering in local woodland."

Crane coughed into his hand, a gentle nudge to Derek that this would be a good time to mention the henna tattoos.

Anderson looked at Crane and his eyes widened in an unspoken question. Crane took the hint and said, "Mr and Mrs Franks, there's something else you need to be aware of before you see Bethany."

"Yes?"

"What is it?"

"She has marks on her arms, drawings and symbols. They've been painted on in henna, so they will fade with time, disappearing altogether eventually, but your daughter is very conscious of them and she's happier keeping her arms covered at times."

"Oh my God, what have they done to my baby?" Mrs Franks fell against her husband in a fit of weeping.

After giving her a few minutes to recover, Crane went on. "I'm afraid that your reaction is precisely why we needed to warn you first, before you meet Bethany. Otherwise seeing them without being prepared would have been such a shock. And you need to be strong for her."

"Am I not allowed to be upset?" Mrs Franks said. "What mother wouldn't be upset, tell me that!"

Mr Franks slid his arm down from where it rested along his wife's shoulders and rubbed his hand in circles on her back.

Anderson said, "Please, Mrs Franks, you must try not to be distressed about them. It's very important that Bethany doesn't see your upset as a rejection of her. For now all she needs is love and acceptance. The rest can come later. Now, if you can compose yourself, we'll take you through to Bethany."

Mrs Franks seemed to find some strength for somewhere deep inside her. She opened her handbag, grabbed a tissue out of it, wiped her eyes and blew her nose. She then took out a comb, pulling it through her short dark hair. Those familiar actions seemed to help ground her, for when she clicked her handbag shut she said, "Alright, I'm ready now."

Crane and Anderson hung back as her parents entered Bethany's room, Mrs Franks going first, with her husband behind. Just before Anderson closed the door to give them some privacy, they heard Bethany utter one word. "Mum."

Thirty Five

Rushed off his feet, with several people waiting for tattoos, Blake didn't take much notice of the man who had just walked through the door.

"Be with you in a minute, mate," he called as he heard the old fashioned ting of the bell announcing those arriving and departing, and then he shouted for his wife who was making coffee in the small kitchen at the back of the shop.

"Mimi, customer," he called as he concentrated on finishing his present client's artwork.

Blake was in the middle of the latest phase of a full sleeve and he couldn't afford to get any of it wrong, as the whole job was worth several thousand pounds to him.

Glancing round he saw that his two co-workers were finishing up, putting dry gauze over the new tattoos and handing out instruction leaflets detailing their after-care. Excellent, that meant two more customer's off the settees where they were waiting and into the chair.

Blake had done well with his business, deliberately siting it in the middle of two housing estates, the local authority kind, not the commuter type. He had a good business antenna and so far it was paying off. He was responsible for the shop, paying the rent, rates and dealing with the bureaucracy that went hand in hand with being a small business owner. He rented out the two 'chairs' which meant that he had a fixed income coming in every week, as well as the takings from his own tattoos.

Finishing the part of the tattoo he'd been working on, he applied the gauze, but dispensed with the advice and thanked the man profusely as he made an appointment to come back in three days to continue the work on his sleeve.

"Right," he looked at the customer's waiting. "Are you next?"

"Clay, you're up," Mimi said. "I've taken his details," she turned to Blake and handed him a welcome cup of tea to take with him back to his booth.

"Okay, mate, what can I do for you today?" he said as Clay stripped his shirt off revealing a few existing tattoos on both arms.

"I want this," he said and thrust a piece of paper at Blake. "At the top of my arm, about here, see? Then I'll come back next week and get another one done on the other arm. I hope you can do freehand. You were recommended as one of the best in the area."

As Blake stared in horror at the symbol before him, badly drawn on a scrappy piece of paper, Clay said, "Here mate, are you alright?"

Blake didn't think he was alright. Not by a long chalk. The sight of the design the man wanted on his arms had made him go faint and hot and cold all at the same time. It was that sulphur sign. The same as before. What the hell was he supposed to do now?

"Yeah, sorry, I'm fine. I've, um, just got to top up the ink, won't be a minute."

Blake disappeared into the back room, well back cubbyhole really, and grabbed a glass from the sink. He filled it with water from the tap and gulped it down. Jesus, another one. What should he do?

The small room went dark as Mimi appeared in the doorway, blocking out the light.

"What the hell's wrong with you," she hissed, so as not to disturb the customers.

"It's that design, the same one, my bloke wants one."

"What design, stop gibbering."

Blake leaned against the sink for support and tried again. "The bloke in my chair wants a sulphur tattoo."

"Christ Almighty. The same one?"

"Near enough, a bit more elaborate than the last, but it's clearly the same symbol."

Mimi delved into her voluminous skirts and brought out her mobile phone.

"What are you doing?" he hissed, grabbing her wrist.

"Phoning the police, of course."

"And lose today's profits? Not likely. There's customers waiting and one in each of the three booths. Calling the coppers will empty this place quicker than a dose of the runs. No. We'll phone them after we close up. You've taken his contact information?"

"Of course, I already told you that," Mimi sniffed.

"Well that'll do then. Now I need to get on." Blake pushed his way past his wife, not an easy thing to do given her size, and returned to his booth.

"You alright now, mate?" Clay asked as Blake took his place on his stool. "Only you don't look too good."

"Oh I'm okay. I've just a bit of a bug, nothing serious, don't worry I'm okay to work." Blake was conscious that he was gabbling. Well he'd have to stop his mouth running away with him and his hands shaking and think of the business. It wasn't anything to do with him who the customer was, or why he wanted that sign tattooed on his arm. The rozzers would just have to wait to pick up the bloke, once Blake had finished with him and pocketed the cash.

***

"You did what?" Blake spluttered at his wife when they'd closed the shop for lunch and they were alone at last. The other two tattooists had gone to the pub, but Blake had declined their invitation to go with them. "You really took a picture of him?"

"Bloody right I did. If you weren't prepared to ring the police right away, then I thought that the least we could do was to give them a photograph of the bloke."

Mimi indicated Anderson and Crane who had gone directly to the shop as soon as they received her phone call, just as Blake had known they would. He was relieved that at least they weren't in uniform and driving a traffic car. But there was no getting away from it you could clock them as police from a 100 yards. There weren't many people on the estates that a) wore suits or b) had conservative haircuts.

"And I'm very pleased that you did," said Anderson to Mimi with reference to the photo. "Why don't you WhatsApp that to me, please," and he handed Mimi his card with his mobile number on it.

"WhatsApp, again, Derek? I'm impressed."

"Shut up, Crane, or I'll knock your stick out of your hands." Turning to Blake, Anderson said, "And you say it was the same sign?"

"Yes, it had a few more fancy bits on it, but it was the same basic design."

"I've got that as well," Mimi chimed in.

"Jesus, woman," Blake admonished his wife.

"Don't fret. I told him that you liked the tattoo so much that you wanted a picture of it, so we could display it and I thanked him profusely for coming to us and for giving you the opportunity to work on his design."

"You never!"

Crane laughed.

"Tickled pink he was and let me take several close ups. Shall I WhatsApp them to you as well Mr Anderson?"

"Um, yes, thanks," The two policemen looked bewildered by Mini as she handed them a piece of paper with Clay's full name, address and telephone number on it. But Blake just laughed. That was his Mimi alright. Always full of surprises.

Thirty Six

"Right, gather round please," Anderson called to the team as he walked to the front of the room. Bullock wondered what the hell Anderson wanted now. Why couldn't he just leave them in peace to do their allotted tasks? The trouble was he was too fond of his own voice. But he supposed he'd better listen.

"A local tattoo artist has reported to us that another man attended his premises and requested a sulphur design tattoo."

Christ, what was coming now? Unfortunately Bullock had an idea what it was and the thought of it was making his stomach feel like a washing machine on the rinse cycle.

DC Douglas pressed a couple of keys on his computer and a photograph flashed up on the wall behind Anderson.

"This is the tattoo the man so proudly asked for."

Bullock was desperate to sit down, but had to stay standing with the rest of the team. So he remained upright, clenching his buttocks as tightly as he could.

"And this is the photograph of the man who had it done. Not as clear an image as I'd have liked, but it gives us a lot to go on."

Bullock groaned and put his arms out onto his desk to keep himself upright. Things were going from bad to worse as Anderson had just shown everyone a photograph of the supplicant, Clay. He had to hold it in. He must. But the more anxious he was as each revelation hit him, the more unsettled his stomach became. The whole of his intestines were rolling around in his belly and he couldn't stop them.

"Now we also have his full name and address, so Crane and I are off to see him. It would have been better, obviously, if the tattoo shop had rung us while he was still there, but at least we have an identification for someone who is definitely a person of interest."

Anderson went on and on, then at last began allocating tasks, which meant that he was near the end of the briefing. Sweat was popping up all over Bullock's face, back and neck. He was beginning to feel like a menopausal woman, going hot and then cold by turn. One moment on fire and the next chilled to the bone. His hands couldn't support his weight much longer, his arms were starting to tremble with the strain and when Anderson at last dismissed them, Bullock collapsed onto his desk. But his relief didn't last long. His stomach was calling and doubled over in pain with his buttocks clenched, Bullock hobbled to the toilets, promising himself that he would find Clay and it better be soon, before Anderson did.

After relieving himself of the day's consumption of coffee, tea and stale sandwiches, he was finally able to think straight. Glancing at his watch, Bullock knew precisely where Clay could be found. And as soon as he could get off the bloody toilet he'd make his way over there.

Thirty Seven

The click, clack of the balls greeted Bullock as he climbed the stairs leading to the snooker club. He couldn't remember the name of it now, but it was located over shops in what could laughingly be called Bordon's high street. As he pushed through the door, there were half a dozen people at the bar, talking in muted tones and five of the eight tables were in use. The atmosphere was a strange mixture of calm, which was energised every now and then by a player potting the ball from a particularly difficult shot. Luckily Clay was at the bar and not at a table, so his presence shouldn't make too much of a mark on the customers.

"Clay," he hissed.

"Hey, what are you doing here? Want a pint?"

"No I don't want a bloody pint," Bullock grabbed Clay's arm. "We need to talk," and he pulled Clay into the toilets, which was a place he'd visited far too often for his liking recently.

"What's with the tattoo?"

"Oh, you heard about that did you? Well, you had one and so I thought I'd get one too, as I'm your assistant like. Want to see it?"

"No I don't want to bloody see it," said Bullock, ignoring the disappointment on Clay's face.

"Well, I suppose it does just look like a big scab at the moment, but it'll be great once that's fallen off."

Bullock stood and stared at Clay. What had he been thinking when he'd decided to use Clay as a general dogsbody? The man was nothing but a bloody idiot. A liability.

"You have not the faintest idea about keeping things quiet have you? Who've you been blabbing to? What did you tell them at the tattoo shop?"

"Now look here, I've not blabbed. I never told them nothing!"

"No, but you got that tattoo and now the police have got you."

"Police? Why? How?"

"Because the tattoo artist recognised the symbol and reported you to the police. They've got your address and your phone number."

Clay pulled out his mobile and looked at it in consternation. Then his face brightened. "I used my old address, not my new one. See, boss, I was thinking, eh?" and he prodded at his temple with his finger.

"Look, trust me, you've got to go into hiding. Go to Tesco or somewhere, buy a burner phone and some supplies and then get your arse out of sight."

Clay's eyes filled with tears. "Where should I go? Are the police really after me? I didn't mean any of it. Those girls, they were an accident. I didn't do it on purpose. Maybe they'll understand once I tell them…"

"Shut the fuck up!" Bullock shouted. "You're not to talk to anyone, especially the police, do you hear me?"

"Yes. Sorry." But Clay still seemed uncertain. "I don't know where to go, where shall I go?"

Bullock thought for a moment, trying to calm his temper as well as his stomach, which had started to churn once more at the smell of the none too clean toilets.

"I know. That car park in Farnborough. The one that no cars can get into. Do you know where I mean?"

"Yeah, on top of the shopping centre."

"Well go up there and find yourself a nice quiet corner. Once you're settled send me a blank text so I know your new number, oh and dispose of your old one."

"Dispose of it?"

"Yes. For God's sake, Clay, wake up will you. They can trace you with that one. Look, let's do it now shall we? And take this card, it's got my mobile number on it so you can text me later."

Bullock grabbed Clay's phone, threw it on the ground and then stamped on it for good measure. The back had fallen off and the battery had come out of its housing, exposing the sim card. Bullock reached down and picked that up, breaking the card in half and dropping it and the remains of the phone in the bin.

"Right, off you go, get a new phone and some supplies and hide out in the car park. Find a nice quiet dark corner. Alright?" Bullock felt he needed to repeat the instructions.

Clay nodded.

"Go on then, we shouldn't be seen leaving together. I'll talk to you later," and Bullock physically pushed Clay out of the door, before rushing into a cubicle and slamming the door behind him.

Thirty Eight

Anderson was grabbing his faithful beige raincoat when DC Douglas appeared at the door.

"You wanted me, guv?"

"Yes," Anderson said shrugging into his coat. "Crane and I are going to Clay Underwood's address and I want you to stay here and see if he's got a record. If not, he may have been called into the station for questioning, or been a witness. Anything. Whatever it is, find it for me. Okay?"

"Yes, guv."

"Oh and Douglas?"

"Guv?"

"Where the hell is DS Bullock?"

"Sorry, I don't know. He just said he had something to do and it couldn't wait."

DC Douglas slipped out of the door and Anderson turned to Crane. "Bloody man's never where he's supposed to be. Oh well, I'll deal with him later. You ready?"

"Yes," replied Crane, but he wasn't at all sure that he was.

His leg was playing up big time now and he was afraid

it was going to collapse under him. He was gripping his stick, hoping it would save him should his leg buckle. He was desperate to hide his problems from Derek. As a soldier, he'd always been urged to give his best, go to the limit and beyond, and therefore it was hard for him to admit when enough was enough. Crane always wanted to go through the physical pain barrier and come out the other side - but this was no race or exercise on the Brecon Beacons. This was Aldershot town and the reality was that if he pushed himself too hard he could do permanent damage to his leg and hip. As he clumped behind Derek towards the car, he realised he might have to say something soon. But not just yet.

Arriving at the block of maisonettes in Farnborough, Crane and Anderson wound their way through the maze of properties, following the signs until they reached the one they wanted. The door was a flimsy looking affair and when Anderson rapped on it, it sounded hollow. Looking around Crane couldn't see any CCTV cameras, just row upon row of sky TV antennas. They heard a shuffling behind the door and the rattle of a chain, before a man poked his head through a small gap.

"Yes?"

"DI Anderson, Aldershot Police," Derek flipped his ID open. "We're looking for Clay Underwood."

"Never heard of him," and the man went to close the door.

"Not so fast," said Anderson, putting his foot in the way to stop the man closing the door. "I suggest you let us in. We're investigating a murder and I'm sure you don't want to be charged with obstructing the course of justice, or even become a suspect."

Crane grinned at the look of fright on the man's face. He had to admit he loved the feeling of power that a badge brought. The chain was quickly taken off the door and the inhabitant of the flat turned and ran back into his den.

The man stood before them in the small, cramped room, which was dominated by a television and stunk of stale cigarette smoke and unwashed clothes.

"Who are you?"

"John Smith."

Crane spluttered and said, "Really?"

"Really."

"Let me see some ID, then."

At Crane's request, the man grabbed a wallet off a small table and took out his driving licence, handing it over.

"Here, Anderson, he really is called John Smith," Crane grinned.

"Well, John Smith," said Anderson, "we're looking for Clay Underwood. We understood he was living at this address."

"Never heard of him," Smith said. "I've been here three years. He might have had the flat before me."

"Any idea where he went," Anderson sighed.

"Why would I know? What am I, his personal assistant?"

At a glare and a threatening step forward from Crane, Smith quickly said, "Sorry. Look, this is a housing association place and there was no sign of any previous tenant when I moved in here."

Anderson walked to the door of the small filthy living room. "You don't mind me looking around do you? Seeing as how you've nothing to hide."

Mr Smith glanced at Crane, who was still glaring at him, and then at Anderson, and shook his head. "Help yourself," he said and then shook a cigarette out of the packet he grabbed off the table. "I'd give you one, but I'm a bit broke, you know?" he said to Crane.

"Nah, you're alright, I've given up."

Anderson returned, saying to Crane, "He's right, there's no one else here. Mr Smith I want the details of the Housing Association you rent from please."

Smith shuffled papers in a cabinet that looked like it was about to collapse and drew one out. Anderson copied out the details and then took a photo of it on his mobile before they left.

Walking to the car, Anderson pulled out his phone and called Douglas. "That's an old address for Clay Underwood, have you come up with anything?"

Crane could hear Douglas' voice as Derek had him on speaker.

"No, sorry, guv, I've not found anything. He seems to be clean. Not even a parking ticket. Which, I guess doesn't help us at all."

"Exactly, it doesn't."

Anderson ended the call and put the phone back in his pocket, and the two men walked back through the buildings.

By now Crane was limping badly. He was having trouble walking back to the car, the pain making him wince. Well more than wince, more like a grimace. He was trying to hide the problems with his leg from Derek and was doing so quite successfully he thought, until he tripped over a tuft of grass of all things and would have fallen if Derek hadn't grabbed him in time.

"I think you should call it a day," Derek said.

Trying to regain his composure, Crane straightened his suit jacket and said, "No, you're all right. I'm fine."

Anderson laughed. "Fine, eh. That's why you look so bloody awful is it? I'd hate to look like that if I was feeling fine."

Crane had to smile. "Well, maybe fine wasn't the best description."

"What do you want to do?"

"To be honest, go home. My head doesn't want to, but the body is screaming otherwise."

"Eminently sensible. Home it is and I'll bring you up to date when I collect you first thing tomorrow. But to be honest I don't really expect us to be anywhere other than where we are now. Bloody nowhere. "

Thirty Nine

Crane was already at home, lying on the settee to rest his leg and hip and not really watching the television that flickered away in the corner of the room, when Tina arrived back home with Daniel.

"Hey you," she smiled and kissed him. "What's this then, half day?"

"Forced upon me, I'm afraid," he said, indicating his leg and trying his best not to sound as pissed off as he felt. After all, none of this was Tina's fault.

"Oh, poor you. Have you taken your pills?"

He nodded his agreement.

"Sure?" she leaned down to look at his face. Tina was well aware that sometimes he didn't take them all.

"Definitely."

"Shit. In that case it's got to be bad. Just let me sort Daniel out and then I'll make us a cuppa."

Crane listened to his wife and son chattering away to each other in the kitchen and not for the first time since his accident, felt left out. If he did try and join them, by the time he'd managed to get himself to the kitchen, Daniel would be going upstairs, or out in the garden and Crane would have missed the moment. Resting in the lounge he felt isolated from his family and he also felt isolated from the team at the police station and from the investigation.

Before the accident he would have become angry with the constraints placed upon him and rant and rave in his frustration. But now his enemy wasn't anger, but fear of being left out, which in turn led to depression. He'd spent months convalescing and waiting for the chance to be part of life again. And now he had that chance, sort of. Would his injuries take that chance away? Rip out his fragile equilibrium and leave him spiralling down into the darkness?

He was still brooding when Tina came back into the room, carrying his mug of tea.

"There you go, super dad," she said, alluding to the mug which Daniel had given him for Father's Day.

"I'm not very super at the moment," Crane grumbled.

"Oh God, one of those days is it? Come on then, spit it out." She sat on the floor, facing him, leaning against the settee he was lying on.

"You don't want to listen to my moaning," he said.

"Yes I do. Now spill."

"It's just that… well… look… how am I supposed to live with this?" he eventually spat out. "Derek had to bring me back early today because my leg kept buckling and my hip is killing me. I tripped over a tuft of grass of all things. Fat lot of use I am to the team."

"Oh, your injuries will take time to heal, Tom. You know they will."

"Well we haven't got much time. We have to find these bastards before another girl is taken. How will I feel if another young girl goes missing or is found dead and I've not been able to work properly because of this bloody stupid leg? How am I supposed to live with that?"

he ended up shouting.

"Why would they want one?"

"Sorry?" Crane tried to calm himself down by taking sips of his hot tea.

"Why would they want another girl? Or come to that why did they want the first two?"

"How do you mean?"

"Well, weren't you looking at a Satanic angle?"

"I know what you're doing," Crane said, narrowing his eyes at her. "You're just trying to take my mind off the pain."

"No I'm not," Tina looked horrified. "I'm interested, Tom, I always have been interested in your work."

"Oh, alright then," and he told her about the Satanic rituals and his theory that they'd wanted the children for a Satanic baptism and then intended to keep them and bring them up in the Satanic Church. "I don't think they want to hurt or abuse the kids, as it's not part of their ethos, strangely enough."

"Have you talked to Anderson about this?"

"Sort of. He told me to go away and look at that angle, but on my own time and I mustn't tell anyone. Not even…"

Tina laughed. "Not even me?"

"That's what he said."

"And have you?"

"Have I what?"

"Done some more research."

Crane saw where she was going. "No I've not."

"Well then maybe you should," she said and stood to take their mugs back into the kitchen.

As he watched her walk away, a grin started to form, hesitantly at first, until he was smiling widely. When she returned he said, "Perhaps I should just take a look on the internet again tonight. You know, before I go in tomorrow. What do you think?"

"I think it's a very good idea."

Forty

Bullock walked into the house and literally collapsed from the stress and pressure. He leaned against the tiny hall wall, holding himself up on the side table with one hand and with the other fumbled for his keys and phone. He dropped them onto the table and then dropped to the floor. Putting his elbows on his knees and his head in his hands, he groaned.

What the hell was he to do? They'd named the girl who'd escaped from them as Bethany somebody or other. Which was all very fine and dandy, but what would happen when she started to remember things? Which she might well do after she was re-united with her parents. Could she identify him? Or Clay? Or both? Did they have their hoods on at all times when they were with her? He just didn't know. He couldn't remember no matter how hard he tried. He wanted to tip on his side onto the floor, roll up into a ball and never have to face the world again. His head was hurting with all the questions that had no answers and his body felt like he'd been repeatedly kicked all over, by large, muscular, hooligans, wearing steel toe-capped boots.

The other biggie was the fact that Clay had been

identified. He couldn't believe the stupidity of his so called 'second in command'. The only thing Clay was in command of was creating chaos. Fancy going to get a bloody tattoo. The bloke was just plain bonkers. He had absolutely no idea of the wider picture. He couldn't see any further than the end of his nose. He was becoming more and more of a liability and Bullock was frightened of what Clay would cock-up next. He'd have to come up with a strategy to keep Clay under control.

He pushed himself up off the floor and went towards the kitchen where Enid was making as much noise as she possibly could, whilst she did what was loosely termed as cooking. Anyone who'd come to dinner and had to eat her food, never came back. The smell permeating the hall from the kitchen wasn't at all enticing, reminding him more of gone off chicken than what he supposed was her chicken casserole. After all it was Thursday. These days she made huge pots of the stuff so she could feed her parents as well as them. The aroma was making him feel sick, or was it his fear? He ran his hand over his cheeks and chin, a kind of girding of the loins before he entered the lion's den.

"Hi," he managed to say, walking over to the fridge and pulling out a bottle of beer.

"Oh, it's you," she said making Bullock wonder who else it might have been.

There was no, 'how are you?' or 'have you had a good day?' just indifference. To be honest he felt the same about her. But it would have been nice to talk to her about his day, explain the pressure he was under; tell her about Anderson picking on him, about how he was having difficulty becoming an accepted member of the team, how he wished they'd never moved, that Clay was nothing but a giant fuck-up, how two young girls threatened to bring him down and expose his predilections and that shortly he was going to be the laughing stock of the Satanic world.

"Dinner will be a bit late," she said. "I've got problems with mum and dad again. Dad fell over the stoop going into the garden, for goodness sake! So I've been to the hospital with him. But first I had to get someone to sit with mum. Then we had to wait for hours once we got there, just for a few bloody stitches. But, obviously, they were concerned about concussion, so I've got to keep an eye on him and I'm not supposed to leave him on his own. That means that after I've made this, I'm going back there tonight, just to make sure, you know?"

Bullock didn't reply. He didn't deem that one was necessary. She didn't really want him to anyway. She was just talking on and on, oblivious as to whether he was listening or not. And, of course, she was talking about her parents. As usual. They were all she ever talked about, all of the time. Looking after them, and then talking about them, was her life.

He wished she'd go and live with the oldies. Make their house her home. But no, she'd rather stay with him, so she could wind him up night after night. His home had become a silent battle ground and he wasn't prepared to put up with it anymore. He realised that he felt that she was nothing more than an annoying guest in his house and what was more, she was so bloody maddening.

He wondered if he could formally cursed her, like their founder Anton LaVey had, against a man called Sam Brody, in response to Brody's jealous threats and attempts to discredit him.

But then he also remembered that LaVey's girlfriend,

the late, great, Jane Mansfield, had been inadvertently killed in a car crash along with the cursed Sam Brody. For on the night of Mansfield's death, LaVey had been clipping a Church of Satan news item from the German magazine, Bild-Zeitung. When he turned the item over to paste it into the press book, LaVey was shocked to see he had inadvertently cut into a photo of Jayne on the opposite side of the page, right across her neck. Fifteen minutes later, a reporter from the New Orleans Associated Press bureau called Anton to get his reaction to a tragic accident. Jayne Mansfield had been practically decapitated when she was thrown through the windshield of the car that she and Brody had been travelling in.

So maybe Bullock needed to heed such a lesson. He best be careful who he cursed. He wouldn't want a curse on Enid to inadvertently ruin anyone else's life.

But as she continued to prattle away, not caring whether he was taking any notice of her, he just wanted to shut her up. Needed to shut her up. His head hurt and he was sweating and his fists were clenching and unclenching. But the bloody bitch was oblivious to him and his problems, she was still going on and on about her sodding parents, and before he knew it he'd pushed her up against the sink where she was washing up, pinning her there with his weight as he leaned against her back. Then his hands were around her throat, throttling her, choking the life out of her, shutting her up for ever.

And it felt so bloody good.

Forty One

The next morning Crane eagerly awaited Anderson's arrival and when he heard the car horn from the car, he opened the door and stood on the front step, gesticulating wildly at his friend.

"Where's the fire?" Anderson shouted through the open car window. "What's the matter? Not ready yet?"

"I'm fine thanks. I just wanted to talk to you before we go to the office."

"Oh, okay, I hope you've got some coffee on then?"

"Sure, come through to the kitchen."

As Anderson sat, Crane asked him how the enquiries with the Housing Association about Clay Underwood had gone.

"Nothing doing," said Anderson, slipping off his raincoat and sitting at the kitchen table. "They won't play ball. Some officious do-goody said we needed a warrant before they'd even see if they've a forwarding address for him."

"Will you get one?" Crane said as he put the coffee on the table between them.

"No, everything we've got on him is circumstantial. Realistically all we have is that he wanted a particular tattoo. That doesn't mean much does it?"

"No, our best bet is to find him."

Anderson said, "But how? The only thing we can do is put his face out to the patrol cars and the neighbourhood police and hope someone sees him."

"Well," said Crane. "While we're waiting, I've done some more research on the Satanic Church. You remember, you asked me to research it at home, in my own time?"

"How is that going to help?" Anderson grumbled, not appearing convinced.

"I think it will help profile who we are looking for. I think we're looking for a Satanic Grotto."

"You what?"

"In the Church of Satan, each local cabal is called a Grotto, which reinforces the hidden and mysterious aspect of the Church of Satan. Grottos are designed to exist organically, solely to serve the specialized interests of a particular association of local members. Chartered Grotto Masters regularly report their activities to Central Office, which by the way is in America and their charters are subject to yearly renewal."

"You've got to be kidding me."

"If only I was. I've also found out the rules they live by, you know a bit like the 10 commandments, only they've got eleven."

Anderson grinned, "That figures."

Crane shared the humour, but then pushed a piece of paper across the table to Derek. "Here they are."

The paper was a print-out from Crane's computer.
.

The Eleven Satanic Rules of the Earth.

Do not give opinions or advice unless you are asked.

Do not tell your troubles to others unless you are sure they want to hear them.

When in another's lair, show them respect or else do not go there.

If a guest in your lair annoys you, treat them cruelly and without mercy.

Do not make sexual advances unless you are given the mating signal.

Do not take that which does not belong to you, unless it is a burden to the other person and they cry out to be relieved.

Acknowledge the power of magic if you have employed it successfully to obtain your desires. If you deny the power of magic after having called upon it with success, you will lose all you have obtained.

Do not complain about anything to which you need not subject yourself.

Do not harm little children.

Do not kill non-human animals unless you are attacked or for your food.

When walking in open territory, bother no one. If someone bothers you, ask them to stop. If they do not stop, destroy them.

"Bloody hell," said Anderson. "I'm not sure what to make of those."

"Well, what I find most interesting is the one that says do not harm little children."

"Why?" Anderson peered at the paper again.

"Well the children haven't really been harmed have they?"

"Come again?" said Anderson.

"Well, they have not been sexually abused, bruised, or

broken in any way. Just used for something, some sort of ritual probably. They've terrified them, yes, but not harmed them."

"What about the dead kid then?"

"I think that may have been an accident," Crane said. "Now all I've got to do is to find this branch of the Satanic Church and the members, to prove my theory."

"No problem, then. Case solved."

"Your sarcasm isn't appreciated," snapped Crane.

"Well excuse me, but finding a branch of the Satanic Church is about as easy as finding Clay Underwood."

Unfortunately Crane had to concede that Anderson had a point.

Forty Two

DS Bullock got ready to leave his house the next morning with a sense of satisfaction of a job well done. He'd been able to get up, drink a cup of tea, have a shower and get dressed, all in wonderful silence. At his own pace, in his own place. Bliss.

Last night after dealing with Enid up, he'd cleaned up the kitchen, chucked out the disgusting chicken casserole and unplugged the phone. Then he'd gone to bed and had the best sleep he'd had in ages.

As he checked he had his wallet and mobile phone with him, he glanced through the kitchen window into the garden and wondered if anyone would notice the newly turned soil in the flower bed at the end of the garden? He held his breath and then let it go. No, there were six foot high fences all around it, so probably not. So he relaxed. But had someone been looking out of their bedroom window in the early hours of the morning? He ground his teeth. Surely not. It wasn't that sort of neighbourhood. Everyone worked. Everyone would be fast asleep at 2am. He would be fine.

If he'd had more time and had planned Enid's death properly, he wouldn't have buried her in the garden. But he wasn't really thinking straight at the time. When he'd seen her lying dead at his feet he'd had to put her somewhere. He couldn't leave the body in the house, it would soon start smelling. He couldn't leave her in the boot of his car, what if DI Anderson wanted driving around? He just hadn't had the energy to drive all the way out to the farm and bury her there. So the garden had had to do. Maybe he'd move her later. Once everything had quietened down.

He looked down at his hands which were full of scratches. He'd just have to hope that nobody noticed them. At least they were clean. He'd managed to scrub all the ingrained dirt and soil from his hands. He should have worn gloves, but he hadn't been thinking particularly clearly.

Doubts continued to plague him as he drove to work, but by the time he walked through the front door of the police station, he was fine. Confident. And anyway he was so bloody relieved that the bitch couldn't nag him anymore that that thought alone put a smile on his face.

"You seem happy this morning, Bullock."

Anderson's voice gave him a start.

"Oh, well, you know, guv, the sun's shining and all that. Better than being miserable, eh?"

Bullock couldn't believe that the first person he met at work was the boss. How typical was that?

"What happened to your hands?"

"Eh?" Bullock was still flustered from meeting Anderson and his brain wasn't working properly as his body flooded with fear.

"Your hands, man. They're all scratched."

"Oh, I'm trying to tame the new garden, as we've just moved in. You know how it is, but gardening isn't my forte." Bullock's mouth was running away with him but he couldn't seem to stop it. "I forgot to put on my gardening gloves when I was pruning the roses."

"Does it seem better now?"

"What?" Bullock felt he was swimming underwater, his limbs were getting heavier and his brain was shutting down.

"The garden?"

"Oh, yes, guv, much better thanks." Bullock managed to get his legs to move and started to edge away from Anderson. "I'll, um, just get a coffee, then get on." Still walking backwards he didn't notice DC Douglas behind him and trod on his toe.

"Hey," Douglas shouted, causing Bullock to stop walking. But he couldn't stop colliding with Douglas, who was holding a full mug of coffee and promptly spilled it all over the floor as Bullock bumped into him.

"Oh, God, sorry, um, I'll get a cloth," and Bullock turned and ran towards the kitchen.

Once there, he grabbed the sink and tried to calm himself down, taking deep breaths.

The flashback took him by surprise.

All of a sudden his head was filled with the image of his wife pushed up against the stainless steel sink in their kitchen, making strange choking noises as he increased the pressure on her throat.

He sprang away from the sink in the toilets, feeling as though the metal of the sink had burned his fingers, and the action seemed to clear the unwanted image from his head. With shaking hands he ran cold water from the tap and put his burning hands underneath it. It would be alright, he kept telling himself. She was gone and couldn't hurt him anymore. No one knew what he'd done. He just had to hold it together. What he'd just told Anderson was true. He had been doing the gardening; only he'd not been pruning the roses, but pulling them up. The worst part was over. He'd got away with it. Things could only get better from here on in.

Forty Three

DS Bullock was still checking the missing person files, when Crane and Anderson called the team to attention. He knew that checking the files was a waste of time, of course, but no one else did, so he was pretty much on automatic pilot. As long as he kept clicking through the records, then he could fool people into thinking he was beavering away at his allotted task.

He looked up from his monitor, irritated at being interrupted, to find Anderson had an image from the overhead projector spread across the back wall. It was a list of some sort. He peered at it, only to remember that he had his reading glasses on. Taking them off, the blur instantly clarified into readable text. It was the Eleven Rules of the Earth. He sat transfixed. Who had found them?

Anderson was prattling away and Bullock caught a name - Crane. That explained it. He'd been wary of Crane finding something like this when he'd taken a look at his search history on his computer and found he'd been looking at pages about Satanic worship. Mind you, he didn't think Crane had seen him do it, but it meant that to a certain extent he was prepared for what they'd found. Or at least he'd thought he would be. Prepared that was. Now he wasn't so sure.

Anderson was talking about profiles, the type of people they were looking for; they would be followers, easily led, prone to accidents, unable to fit into normal society, oddballs. He felt the anger rising within him at being described so glibly. They had no idea what they were talking about. How dare they ridicule his beliefs? His rituals?

"You all right?" a voice hissed next to him.

He turned to see DC Douglas, looking at him and questioning him yet again. Why couldn't everyone just leave him alone? "Of course I am, why?" he snapped.

"Because you've just broken yet another pen."

Bullock looked at his hands. They were covered in blue ink and the plastic casing of the pen itself was cracked and broken.

"I was listening and concentrating, alright? Which is what you should be doing?" he hissed back, unleashing his anger at the stupid young man.

By the time Crane and Anderson had finished their briefing, Bullock was sweating so much that he had large damp patches under his arms, discolouring his shirt.

"Are you sure you're okay?"

It was that idiot Douglas again.

"Only you look ill."

Bullock was saved by his mobile phone. Turning away from Douglas he answered it and a croaky, wavering, elderly voice said, "Hello? Hello? Is anyone there?"

It was his father-in-law. "Yes, George. What do you want?"

"Where's Enid? She's not come. She didn't come last night and she's still not here. Where is she? What you have done with her?"

"Nothing." Bullock wanted to add, 'you stupid old man' but stopped himself just in time.

"I need help with mother," the tremulous voice wouldn't stop. "Mother has soiled herself and I can't clean her up. Where's Enid?"

Bullock ended the call in disgust. Cleaning up soiled knickers was a gross thought. Enid had a lot to be grateful to him for. At least he'd saved her from all that crap.

Forty Four

At Crane's insistence, he and Anderson had taken a short stroll outside to the nearest coffee shop. "I need an infusion of real coffee," he'd declared. "I can't think straight without my regular caffeine fix."

It was with a great deal of satisfaction that Crane sank into a chair and picked up his coffee. He was just savouring the delicious, full-bodied aroma, when he was interrupted.

"Guv?"

Someone had spoken to Anderson.

Lifting his eyes, but not his nose, Crane saw the young civilian analyst attached to the team, Holly somebody or other.

"Mind if I join you?"

Crane was just about to say that they were having a break and couldn't it wait, when the young girl went on.

"I've something I need to tell you about and I didn't want to do it in the office."

She glanced over her shoulder and seemed pleased with what she saw, as her shoulders relaxed a little.

"Come on, then," said Anderson. "Sit down. Want a coffee?"

Crane groaned inside. He'd wanted just a few moments away from the case, but it seemed it wasn't to be.

"No, thanks, I only drink green tea," she replied, which didn't surprise Crane in the least. Her brown shoulder length hair was pulled into two plaits. Nothing strange about that. But when you added a startling blue fringe and pink sides, it started to look rather avant-garde. Her long sleeved tee-shirt in muddy green matched her many pocketed cargo pants. She was painfully thin and rather studious in her large framed glasses. She pulled out a chair and sat down. And didn't speak.

"Well?" Crane asked before taking a sip of the elixir that was his flat latte with extra sugar.

"I've found an anomaly in the missing person's database, boss."

"Anomaly?" echoed Anderson.

"Something that shouldn't be there."

"Ah," said Anderson knowledgably, but Crane knew better. His friend was a computer dinosaur.

"What I think has happened is that someone looked at an entry in the data base and deleted it."

Now that was something that even Anderson could understand, thought Crane. Both men leaned forward to listen, Crane's coffee momentarily forgotten.

"I found it when I was checking the data at the end of the day yesterday."

"Who deleted it?"

"Don't know, boss. All I know is that it was done. Here's what was deleted and when," and she handed Anderson an envelope.

He looked uncomprehendingly at the address written on it and the stamp stuck above it.

"It's a ploy, sir. Nothing but a decoy, in case the person who deleted the record saw me going after you. I thought it would look better if I seemed to be going to the post-office.

Anderson grinned. "We'll make a detective out of you yet, Holly."

But he wasn't grinning when he read the entry. Passing it to Crane he said to Holly, "Get back to the office. This meeting never happened, right?"

"Right, sir. Thanks," and she melted away into the crowd.

Crane looked at the piece of paper. It was the entry of a missing child from Birmingham. The image staring at him from the piece of paper was the young girl currently residing in the morgue at Frimley Park Hospital. Crane picked up his coffee but putting it to his lips realised that it had lost its allure.

"Back to the office?" he said struggling with his stick and his chair, but Anderson was already up and away, leaving Crane to limp in his wake.

Within 10 minutes they were back in Anderson's office, looking into the eyes of DC Douglas, trying to decide if he was telling the truth or not.

"It wasn't me, sir; it must have been someone else. I'd never do such a thing. What reason would I have for not finding out who a dead child was? To do something like that would be the end of my career."

Douglas was gabbling, his mouth running away with him, but Crane couldn't see guilt in the man's eyes, only confusion.

After a moment, Anderson dismissed Douglas and picked up the phone. Before dialling he turned to Crane.

"It wasn't him, was it?"

"Nah, normally someone put in that sort of situation

who is guilty, would display symptoms of fear; sweating, dilated pupils, fidgeting. But I didn't see any of that. All I saw was confusion and a desperate plea for us to believe him."

Anderson nodded his agreement.

Crane said, "This isn't good is it?"

Anderson shook his head and Crane looked out of the window of the office at the team working away and wondered who the Judas was. The obvious choice was DS Bullock. But how could they prove it? And what reason would he have for doing it?

Forty Five

Anderson rang the contact number on the data entry sheet detailing the missing person's report for Dawn Davis. As Anderson talked to the police in Birmingham, Crane pulled the sheet towards him and studied it again. Dawn had gone missing a mere week ago, last seen at the Dr Barnardos Home where she was temporarily living. The alarm had been raised when she'd failed to turn up for tea one day. A search of the building had confirmed that she was missing and the police had been informed.

By the time Crane had got to the end of the report, Anderson had finished on the phone.

"Are we going to brief the team now?" Crane asked.

"Not just yet, I want to speak to the person in charge at the Dr Barnardos home first."

Once Anderson had got the correct person, he put the call on speaker.

"Mr Lowe, you're on speaker with DI Anderson and Tom Crane from Aldershot CID. I wonder if you could talk to us about Dawn Davis, please."

"Oh, yes, very unfortunate that," said Mr Lowe. "Have you found her? Is that why you're ringing?"

Crane thought it was more than unfortunate that

Dawn had gone missing, but kept that thought to himself.

"Let's just say we're looking at a new angle on the case. I take it you haven't found Dawn?" Clearly Anderson's brusque tone meant that he wasn't impressed with the supervisor either.

"No I'm afraid not. She's still missing."

"Has she run away before?"

"Oh dear no. She's a lovely girl, comes from a nice family."

"So why was she with you?" Crane butted in.

"Her father is in the Navy and away on exercise at the moment. As her mum is having post natal depression problems after having a little boy, Dawn is…was… here for a few weeks while mum sorted herself out."

"Did she seem okay with that arrangement?"

"Absolutely, she knew it was just temporary while mum was ill."

"How come you lost her?" Crane couldn't help himself.

"This isn't a prison. The children are allowed out at times. But when she went missing it wasn't one of those allotted times. But if a child really was determined to get out, well then she could. The children's favourite place to go is the nearby park. We think she could have gone there. Look, we're all very worried about her, do you know what happened to her?"

"I'm sorry, I've not got any more information at the moment. Thank you for your help and I'm sure someone will be in touch when we have more news."

Derek cleared the call.

"It looks like we've got her then," said Crane. He'd pulled a picture of the dead girl in the morgue to him and was looking at the two photos side by side and pushed them over to Anderson. "What are you going to do now?"

"Brief the team."

"What about our rogue policeman? We still don't know who he or she is."

"We'll just have to take the chance that whoever it is won't interfere in this part of the investigation."

"And meanwhile we'll keep a close eye on them all."

"Absolutely, come on, let's go. I need to get Douglas to print out the file that Birmingham are sending over and the rest of them need to get on the phones and ring any witnesses who were in the nearby park that day. Someone, somewhere knows something, it's just that they don't realise it yet. Birmingham CID are going to tell the parents. Christ knows what it will do to her mum, especially as she's already mentally unstable."

Forty Six

DC Douglas loved his job. He was still very much on probation, he knew that, and he also knew that he was still having difficulties getting on with everyone. Well, getting on with DS Bullock actually. Everyone else seemed alright. Anyway, he guessed what mattered was whether the Guvnor liked him and DI Anderson seemed to so far.

Tasked with going through a pile of witness statements from Birmingham and feeling like an erstwhile Indiana Jones, he dived in. His brain was his hat, which he set at a jaunty angle. His eyes his whip, which he flicked back and forth over the words. His satchel was his notebook, where he jotted down things of interest taken from the statements. He was just waiting until he found that kernel of gold. The one piece of information that could crack the case wide open.

Realising he was spending too much time fantasising and none actually reading the statements in front of him, Douglas chided himself for his over-active imagination and bent to the task.

The office was quiet, with only the occasional ringing of the telephone to disturb it. Everyone was concentrating on their allotted tasks and Douglas felt the weight of the team's tension and anticipation on his shoulders. A huff of annoyance came from DS Bullock, whose desk was opposite Douglas'.

"Anything, boss?" Douglas asked him, sitting up and arching his back to stretch it.

"Nah, bloody waste of time this is. Just loads of people who say absolutely nothing. "

"Well, you never know. Someone could have seen something relevant. Don't you find it exciting?"

"Exciting?"

"Yeah, you know, I bet one of us will find something that could really help the case. Make a difference, you know?"

"I can tell you've not been in this job very long," grumbled Bullock. "You haven't yet realised that most police work is boring, laborious, and totally pointless, not to mention irrelevant."

"Surely not."

"Definitely." Bullock pushed his chair away from the desk. "Fuck it, I'm off for a fag and a coffee."

Douglas looked at Bullock's retreating back wondering when the man had become so cynical and hoped that he would never end up like his DS. He doubted he would. He was a glass half full kind of person and Bullock was clearly a glass half empty; the difference between being a pessimist and being an optimist.

Douglas turned back to the statement on his desk. It was from a woman who had been identified as being in the park on the day that Dawn had disappeared. She was a regular visitor who walked her dog there most days. Douglas wondered if she'd seen Dawn.

- I was walking in the park that afternoon as I usually do, but I can't remember ever having seen the child you are looking for.

Oh well, maybe this one didn't hold the nugget of gold. He nearly dismissed the rest of the statement when his eye caught the words – *ice cream van*. Pulling the paper back towards him, he read on.

- The only thing I can remember seeing that was different that day, was the ice cream van. It wasn't the usual one. I know it was different because the usual one has blue writing on it and this one was red. It had some sort of Italian name and it rang the tune, you know the one that they all ring….

Douglas read the words again. Bloody hell. An ice cream van. And not only that, but an ice cream van that was different. An ice cream van that shouldn't have been there. Douglas sat for a moment, savouring his find, then realised what he was doing. Wasting precious time. This could break the case open. He stood up so suddenly that his chair fell over, but he ignored it and ran towards DI Anderson's office. On the way he barrelled into Bullock who was returning to his desk.

"Hey, can you be a bit more careful? Where's the fire?"

"Sorry, boss. But I've only bloody found it. Got to see the DI," he threw over his shoulder and skidded into Anderson's office.

"Yes, DC Douglas?" Anderson didn't seem particularly happy at being interrupted.

"Have you forgotten that it's usual to knock before entering the office?" Jesus, Crane wasn't very happy with him either. Never mind, they'd love him soon.

"I've found it, guv." Douglas held up the witness statement.

"Found what?"

"A clue. The clue. The nugget of gold."

"God save me from young police detectives," Anderson glanced upwards at the ceiling. Looking back at Douglas, he said, "Now sit down, lad, take a deep breath and tell me what the hell is going on."

Anderson quickly realised that what was going on was potentially a break in the case, but he curbed his own enthusiasm in order to bring his young DC down from the ecstatic state he seemed to be in.

"Well done, lad," he said. "But it's only the start of something, not the end."

"Eh?"

"Explain it to him, Crane, would you?" Anderson said as he turned away and started rummaging in the bottom drawer of his desk. He was sure he had something nice to nibble on somewhere in the midst of the detritus that he always seemed to collect and never seemed to sort out.

"You've got a lead, son," said Crane. "What is more important than the information you've gleaned so far, is what you do with it now."

"Ah, okay, so now I need to find the van."

"Exactly," said Anderson, his voice muffled by the desk. "And how are you going to do that?" he finished as he straightened in his chair and put two Waggon Wheel chocolate biscuits on his desk with some satisfaction.

"Um, call every ice cream firm that operates in that area until I find one with red sign writing?"

Crane said, "Precisely. As it seems our witness saw a working van, find any vans with Italian sounding names and see if they had a van working in that area on the day Dawn disappeared and at about the time our witness saw it."

DC Douglas made to leave, but Anderson called him back. "You can do that after you've made us a cup of tea to go with these chocolate biscuits."

DC Douglas hesitated, as though not sure if Anderson was being serious.

"I take two sugars," said Crane.

"Right, yes, um," and Douglas disappeared as Anderson and Crane tried not to laugh out loud.

"Getting him to make a cup of tea first wasn't nice," commented Crane.

"I needed a way of bringing him down from his euphoria. Otherwise he'll not do the research properly in his haste and he could miss something vital."

"Nice lad though."

"Oh definitely, I reckon he'll go far."

"Is he part of this graduate recruitment scheme?"

Anderson nodded. "It means he'll be fast tracked through the ranks if his results are good."

"So that's why you let him follow up the ice cream van lead, rather than getting someone more senior to do it, such as DS Bullock."

Anderson cringed at the mention of his new DS' name. "I'm still not sure about that bloke. You know, I trust young Douglas more than I do Bullock. There's just something about him, but I can't put my finger on it."

Forty Seven

DS Bullock was scowling at DC Douglas. Douglas could feel his eyes on the top of his head and was determined not to look up. Bullock appeared to want to disrupt Douglas' task and he wasn't sure why.

"So this woman says she saw an ice cream van near the park?" Bullock asked.

Douglas sighed and raised his head. "Yes, I've told you that already."

"But she doesn't know what the name of it was."

"No. So I've got to try and find it, if you'll leave me alone."

"Could be a waste of time."

"Why?" Douglas tried not to sigh and lifted his eyes from his monitor.

"Because witnesses can't be trusted. You'll learn that with experience."

"And that's your experience is it?"

"Yes. So I wouldn't get too excited. As I said it'll probably be a big waste of time."

"Well, waste of time or not, I've been asked by the DI to investigate so…"

Douglas was saved from being rude to his superior

officer by Bullock's phone ringing. He didn't know who was calling the DS, but heard him hiss into the phone, something like, "I keep telling you not to call me…" but the rest was lost as Bullock barged out of the office. Relieved, Douglas picked up his own phone. He couldn't for the life of him figure his DS out. One minute he was fine, the next cynical, then angry; it was making Douglas' head spin.

Looking at his search results for ice cream vans in the Birmingham area, he found one called Galletto's, whose logo included their name in bright red letters, written in a script style. Douglas knew he really should start at the top of the list, not half way down, but he just had a feeling about the name and the logo. Grabbing his phone he called the number.

"Galletto's," a female voice answered. "How may I help you today?" A bit too American for Douglas' taste, but what the hell. At least she was polite.

"Hello, I'm DC Douglas from Aldershot Police. Could I speak to the proprietor please?"

"Police?" the voice squeaked, all pretence at efficiency and customer service gone.

"Yes, from Aldershot in Hampshire."

"Oh, well you want me dad, but he's, he'll be here in a minute. Can you hang on?"

"Sure," he said. "But this is a matter of some urgency."

Douglas was unsure if she'd heard that last bit as the phone clattered down on her desk, which was a pity as he was rather pleased with that phrase, he'd have to use that again.

"Hello," a male voice said.

"Ah, Mr, er, Mr Galletto?"

"No, that's just the company name."

"Oh, right, sorry."

"The name's Walton. What can I do for you?"

"It's about an ice cream van that was seen in the vicinity of Trinity Park in Edgbaston on Thursday 10th March."

"Really? That's not one of my patches. Sorry I can't help you."

Douglas wasn't about to let Walton, or Galletto, or whatever his name was, get away that easily. He said, "Oh, it's just that someone identified the name on an ice cream van seen there as one of yours," Douglas stretched the truth just a little bit. "Can you explain that?"

"Um…"

"Is there any way it's possible that one of your vans was operating outside your patch?"

"Ah, well," Walton hesitated.

"This is a matter of some urgency," Douglas said. "But if you're not prepared to answer my questions, then I'll have to get the local police to call in and see you. Perhaps they can persuade you to help us."

"No, wait… I had a van stolen."

"Stolen?"

"Yes, a couple of months ago now."

"But I didn't find a report of any stolen vans," said Douglas.

"Well no you wouldn't do, as I didn't report it."

"Why ever not?"

"Because of the insurance. It was an old one that I wasn't really supposed to use on account of the insurance having expired, so I never claimed. I didn't want to get into any trouble, get people thinking I'd been using vans with no insurance, like. So I swallowed the loss."

"In that case I need the full details of the van that was stolen and a picture of it if I can. I need to know when and from where it was stolen, registration number, vin number, you name it, I need it," finished Douglas having run out of ideas for questions.

"Alright," said Walton, "just hang on and I'll get the file."

Walton was as good as his word and gave Douglas all the information he needed. When he took it to the SIO, Anderson told him to put in a request for any automated registration number sightings of the van over the past two months. The information was promised for first thing the next morning, enabling Douglas to leave on time that afternoon and down a few well deserved pints in his local pub by way of celebration.

Forty Eight

There were three people who were definitely not celebrating later that day. Crane and Anderson stood in the viewing room of the morgue at Frimley Park Hospital and looked at the man who was with them. Able Seaman Davis was a young man in his late 20's, straight of back and short of hair, and who was turning his cap over and over in his hand. He was in naval uniform, having come to the hospital straight from his ship.

"You've been given compassionate leave?" Crane asked him.

Davis managed a nod and kept fiddling with his cap. He was squeezing it, crushing the fabric between two meaty hands.

"How is your wife?" Anderson asked. Davis turned to look at him with hollowed eyes.

"Not good. She wasn't good before, but now the doctors are recommending she goes into the local psychiatric hospital. Instead of getting help, she's insisting on staying home. She's terrified of letting the baby out of her sight. Convinced he's going to be abducted, just like Dawn was."

Crane had a modicum of understanding of how both

Davis and his wife must be feeling. Tina had suffered with post-natal depression after the birth of Daniel and it had taken months of tablets, doctor's visits and the help of the Garrison community to get her well again. If anything had happened to Daniel during that awful time, neither Tina nor he would have forgiven themselves. It would have blighted the rest of their lives.

"We thought she'd be safe at Dr Barnardos," Davis mumbled to the floor. "I had to stay with my ship and Dawn's parents are dead. We didn't know what else to do."

Anderson gently touched Davis on the arm. "Are you ready?"

"No. But let's do it. I have to get this over with."

Anderson pressed a discreet button by the side of the window and the curtains opened. The eyes of all three of them were drawn to Dawn's lifeless face. She had been a pretty little thing with a small nose sporting a sprinkling of freckles. The sound of someone choking prompted Crane to look back at Davis, who was buckling at the knees, grunts and groans coming from deep within him. Grabbing the man's arm, Crane signalled to Anderson to close the curtain and then they held Davis up as they moved to the seats pushed up against the back wall.

Davis was having trouble breathing and was swaying in his seat, so Crane pushed the man's head between his legs and encouraged him to take slow, deep breaths.

Once Davis had a modicum of control, he lifted his head, scrabbled in his pocket and pulled out a hankie. He wiped his eyes and blew his nose, finishing with a blow of breath. "Okay. Sorry."

Anderson said, "Seaman Davis, was that your daughter Dawn."

Davis nodded.

"I'm sorry but you need to say it out loud."

There was another audible blow of breath, before Davis said, "Yes, that's Dawn."

"Thank you."

"What happens now? Can I take her home with me?"

"Not just yet, the Pathologist has yet to release her body."

"In that case, I'll wait here," said Davis.

"It could take some time," Crane explained gently.

"I've nowhere else to go. There's nowhere else I'd rather be," Davis spoke equally quietly, settling in his seat and staring at the window with the closed curtains, which just a moment ago had framed, like a picture, the body of his daughter.

Forty Nine

"Right, listen up."

Everyone obeyed Anderson's call and came together at the front of the incident room. Yawning, gulping down coffee and leaning against desks and filing cabinets, they all turned their bleary eyes towards their SIO, wondering why he'd called them in so early in the morning.

Anderson was glad to have some news to break to the team. Day after day there had been little to go on and after witnessing the devastating grief of Seaman Davis yesterday, Anderson needed all the good news he could get. The strain on his team was clearly visible. Their faces looked dirty with fatigue and their eyelids blinked rapidly as though trying to wash the cobwebs of tiredness away that were gumming up their eyes.

"I know you've all been working unusually long hours," he began. Everyone nodded their agreement to that. "Well, it looks like our hard work is paying off."

Anderson's quiet sentence ran around the room like an electric current, straightening shoulders, opening eyes, making downturned mouths smile. The only one who didn't look pleased was DS Bullock, Anderson noted.

Instead of being pleased, he looked shocked. His eyes widened and his grip on the chair he was leaning on tightened. Anderson had seen that look before; on the faces of defendants as they were waiting for the judge to pronounce sentence. Or on suspects being caught red handed. Whichever scenario applied to Bullock, Anderson and Crane would have to keep an eye on him.

"DC Douglas has made a major breakthrough in the case. He's found an ice cream van that was stolen a couple of months ago from a Birmingham firm called Galletto's. We've had it shown to the witness who remembered seeing an ice cream van on the day that Dawn was taken from Birmingham and she has confirmed that that's the one she saw."

"Bloody hell."

"Excellent work,"

"Way to go, newbie."

Anderson let Douglas have his few seconds in the spotlight, before continuing. "So, overnight we ran the registration number through the automated number plate recognition system and we've got a list of all the sightings by date. Crane here has the breakdown 'to do' lists, so grab one from him and get on with plotting the route the van took on each date. In the meantime Crane and I will follow up with the Birmingham Police and see if they can identify from their local knowledge, anywhere where the van might be stored. Okay, dismissed, let's get on with it."

As his team jostled for position, lining up to grab a pack of information from Crane, Anderson noted that instead of following his colleagues, DS Bullock left the room. Anderson, who was by now convinced that there was definitely something off with his DS, followed him, and as he left the incident room, he saw the door to the toilets swing shut.

Anderson quietly opened the door to the men's toilets to hear someone retching repeatedly, before flushing a toilet. Anderson timed his entrance as Bullock left the cubicle and the two men met in the middle of the space.

"You alright, DS?" Anderson asked, although it was very clear that he wasn't. Bullock's pasty white forehead was sheened with sweat, his hands were shaking and his legs seemed unable to hold him. He staggered drunkenly to the sinks where he held on tight.

"Sorry, guv, not feeling so good today. Must be something I ate."

"You sure? I hope it's nothing contagious."

"No, just a dodgy prawn sandwich. I'll be alright in a bit," and Bullock leaned over the sink and splashed his face with cold water.

"Well, if you're sure?"

Bullock nodded his agreement and Anderson had no alternative but to take the man's word for it. But he didn't believe him. Not for a minute.

Fifty

Crane had to admit that over the last few hours, they had made enormous progress. The van, on its various journeys, had seemed to start and end at an area in a Birmingham suburb with lock up garages. The CCTV had shown it driving into the street housing the garages, but hadn't captured the exact one it was parked in. The Birmingham Police had investigated and working on the premise that a vehicle used to snatch children would have extra security on the garage it was stored in, had identified three possible garages.

The phone on Anderson's desk rang and Derek snatched it up.

"Ah ha," he said. "Mmmm, alright," he continued, before replacing the receiver.

"Well?" Crane's voice was as sharp as the bolts of pain currently firing down his leg. "What's happening?"

"A friendly local Judge has just signed a Search Warrant for forced entry into the three garages," said Anderson.

"Thank God for that," Crane said putting his leg up on a chair and rubbing his thigh.

"Come on then," Anderson stood.

"Where?"

"To the communications room. Quickly."

"Alright, just let me take a couple of pain killers first," and Crane dry swallowed them as he limped after Anderson. He was beginning to feel like the mermaid in the Hans Christian Andersen tale, the one who wanted to be human. Her wish was granted, and her tail was split in two to form legs. But every step she took was excruciating agony. That just about summed him up, he decided as he limped after Anderson, trying to push the pain from his mind.

The room they entered was dim, populated with people sat at desks, mesmerised by the large computer monitors in front of them.

"Nearly ready," an operator said to Anderson.

"What are we waiting for?" hissed Crane, as he tried to balance himself with his stick.

"Okay, guv, we're up."

"This," said Anderson and indicated the large screen on the wall.

The screen hissed and flickered for a few moments, before clearing to provide a view of a row of lock up garages.

"Is that?" Crane said.

"Yes, the Birmingham police ready to break into the lock ups. One of the officers is wearing a webcam so we can see what's happening."

"Nice," Crane nodded. "Saves a trip up there."

"Exactly."

The picture wobbled as the officer began walking with his team to the first garage. For a moment the screen was filled with the back of a police officer working with bolt cutters to free the locks. They could hear the scuffle of feet, the sound of deep breathing and then, at last, the creak and groan of a metal spring as the door sprang open.

By torchlight, they could see… that the garage was empty.

"Fuck," came the expletive from Birmingham. "Next one."

Crane and Anderson watched as the operation was repeated, with the same result.

"Jesus," Crane's frustration exploded. "Don't say we've got it wrong."

"Have faith, Crane," cautioned Anderson as the officers turned to the third garage.

Once again the screen was filled with the broad blue-cladded back of the officer with the bolt cutters. There were one, two, three cracks of metal breaking and then a rattle as the door rolled upwards.

"Bingo!" someone shouted.

"Out of my way then," said the officer with the camera and the view cleared of bodies to reveal an ice cream van.

Fifty One

Bullock didn't need to look in the mirror to see how awful he looked. He knew his fear could be seen in the sweat on his brow, the trembling of his hands and the shaking of his legs. It seemed to be rolling off him in waves and he was sure everyone could see it; a black fog swirling around his head, rendering him incapable of rational thought. It had been bad enough when they'd identified the dead girl. But it had transpired that that had been the least of his worries. For it was the evidence the Birmingham police had collected from the ice cream van that he was most afraid of. His leg bounced up and down rapidly under his desk as he thought about what had been found.

They'd got the discarded blanket that the girls had been wrapped up in. They'd found the stash of ketamine used to tranquilise the girls and of course the fingerprints. They were everywhere. The rational part of his brain realised that it could take days to sort the evidence out and identify his associate. But the irrational one, the dominant side for the moment, was convinced that the end was near. He considered flight. But where would he go? What would he do for money? Everything he had was tied up in the house. Maybe he could get a quick sale? Maybe he could delay some of the evidence coming to light? They hadn't found the white van used to transport the girls, they hadn't found the secret meeting place, they hadn't found Clay…

That was it. Clay. He had to get rid of Clay. Clay was the one who had done the abductions. Clay was the one who had let one girl escape. Clay was the one who had given the second girl an overdose. Clay was the one person who could identify Bullock.

Bullock's body flooded with relief and he almost fell off his chair as he relaxed. There was a way out after all. Clay was his way out. He wouldn't need to do a runner. But he would still need to put a plan in place that would ensure his disappearance. He'd put the house on the market as soon as he could, change his name, empty his bank accounts… yes it could be done. As long as Clay was out of the picture.

He reached under his desk and grabbed his briefcase, which was mostly used for effect. He'd wanted to portray the organised, dedicated detective and a briefcase said all of those things. It also hinted that every night he was taking work home with him, earning brownie points from the governor. Of course he wasn't any of those things, nor did he do any of those things. He went to work, did as little as possible whilst there and then went home at night with never a second thought for the cases he was working on.

Popping open the clasps of the case, he took out a burner phone and put the briefcase back under his desk. He was just pushing himself out of his office chair when DC Douglas said, "Off somewhere?"

"Just phoning the missus."

"Don't forget your phone then," Douglas nodded

towards the smart phone on Bullock's desk.

"Ah," Bullock said, looking at the burner phone in his hand. "We use a different phone to communicate. Can't abide her tying up my work phone."

Bullock hurried away after blurting out the lie, but he was sure Douglas' eyes were still on him. He could feel them following him all the way to the door.

Once in the men's toilets and after checking that no one else was lurking in a cubicle, he flipped open the phone and called the only number in it.

"Mm,"

"Clay?" Bullock hissed.

"Yeah," Clay drawled. "What do you want? I was asleep. You just woke me up."

"Well, very soon lack of sleep is going to be the least of your worries."

"Eh? What?"

"We need to meet. Soon."

"Alright," Clay didn't sound very excited about the idea. "If you say so."

"I do say so. Meet me at the farm."

"Why so far away? Don't know if I've got enough petrol."

"For fuck's sake, stop moaning and just do as you're told. I'll see you there at 5 pm."

Bullock closed the phone to end the call and placed his hands on the white porcelain sink. The unyielding, cold surface was just what he needed. For that's what he would be. Cold. Unyielding. In control. Very soon Clay wouldn't be a threat, just a distant memory.

Fifty Two

Clay had eventually arrived at the farm where their Satanic meetings took place, after making Bullock wait for 15 minutes, most of which he'd spent pacing around the property and constantly looking at his watch. Bullock had found the farm through a friend of a friend, who knew of an agent wanting to get the place off his books. The old man who'd owned it had died and they'd couldn't finalise the estate until it was sold. As a result Bullock had got it for a song and had paid for it in cash out of the proceeds of the sale of his house near Birmingham. He'd spun the wife a tale about not getting as much out of the sale as he thought they would, and blamed the smaller house down south on the increased property prices in the area. When he'd bought the farm he'd been careful enough to put the property in his wife's maiden name. The floors were creaky, the roof leaked, some windows were broken and from the back, the house appeared to be sliding down a slight incline. Bullock wasn't bothered about any of those things, for the house had a cellar which was cool, dry and large, running under the whole of the house.

Bullock watched from inside the farmhouse as Clay

dragged himself out of the van and clomped over to the house in the black biker boots that he favoured. Christ knew why he liked them, for as to his knowledge Clay had never owned or even ridden on a motorbike. His boots raised the dust on the path and then threatened to break some of the floorboards of the wooden veranda as he stomped around on it. Going outside to meet Clay. Bullock was repulsed by the man's dirty clothing and hair that was matted and greasy.

"Well? What's the matter? Why have you dragged me all the way out here?" Clay was clearly not in the best of moods, which was fine, because neither was Bullock.

"Because they've found the ice cream van," Bullock said, wanting to add 'you moron' but thought better of it.

Clay's attitude quickly changed from sullen to frightened. "Oh shit."

"Exactly."

"I thought you were supposed to stop them doing that?"

"I'm only one man, Clay. I can only hide so much. Someone else in the office found the van and there was nothing I could do to stop it."

"So what happens now?"

"Well now there is a forensic team crawling all over it. They've found your ketamine stash and the blanket you wrapped the girls in and, of course, your finger prints will be all over it."

Clay began pacing up and down the wooden boards, running his hand through his hair and Bullock very much hoped Clay wouldn't touch him with that filthy hand. The tangled mess of hair looked like an open invitation for every bug and insect small enough to make their home in it. The thought of fleas and nits making their home in Clay's hair made Bullock scratch his own head.

Clay stopped pacing and confronted Bullock. "What shall we do?"

"We don't need to do anything. But you have to get away, that's for sure."

"Do you think that's best?"

"Of course I do. It's all very well identifying you, but if they can't find you, then you'll be fine."

"But, but, where should I go? I don't know anywhere else. I've lived here all my life." Clay grabbed at Bullock's jacket. "Help me! You've got to help me!"

Bullock smiled inside, careful not to let it show on his face. He loved it when a plan came together. Forcing himself to put his arm around Clay's shoulders, he said to the unsuspecting man, "I'd been thinking about that while I waited for you. I've got an idea. Here, come inside, I've got something that I think can help," and Bullock moved away from the door so that Clay could go inside first. Once the big man had his back turned to Bullock, he picked up the wooden slat he'd found in the garden. Sturdy and thick, it had several rusty nails protruding from it. It was just what Bullock had been looking for to help Clay on his way to somewhere where he'd never be found.

***

Bullock was in a much brighter mood on the way back from the farm. He might be a bit sweaty and dirty - all that dragging and rolling up a dusty rug hadn't been good for his suit - but all in all he felt that he was back in control. Clay had weighed rather more than Bullock had thought he would. He supposed it was something to do with Clay being a dead weight and he grinned at the pun.

He relived the moment when Clay had walked inside the farmhouse. All it had taken was one good swing from the piece of wood to make Clay tumble to the floor. As his head had banged down, the nails had pierced his skull, meaning that the wooden slat was securely fastened to his head. Bullock hadn't bothered to try and take it out and had just rolled him up in the carpet with it still in situ and dragged him outside onto the verandah. He'd backed up his car to the steps and then tipped Clay into the boot.

After a quick stop at an unsupervised rubbish tip, Bullock drove back to Aldershot with the windows open and the car radio tuned to Jazz FM. It was his favourite radio station and the one that his wife had hated the most. He was beginning to find out how truly liberating it was to be on his own. No nagging wife. No grovelling assistant.

He was just thinking that his life had at last turned a corner, and that the only way was up, when his mobile phone began buzzing in his jacket pocket. Pulling off the road, just in case it was work calling, he stopped the car and looked at the screen. His good mood dissolved in an instant. The call was from his wife's parents. As the mobile buzzed angrily at Bullock, he wondered why they wouldn't stop pestering him. They were constantly asking for him to help them since his wife had mysteriously disappeared from their lives. They were starting to think that Enid's illness, which meant she was unable to see them, was suspicious. Their frail voices warbled through the phone, moaning at him, asking what they should do about this, that and the other. Carping on that they needed help. Just like Clay. I need help. We need help. Everybody fucking needed his help.

Well he was sick of it. Sick of it all, sick of them both and he threw the mobile onto the passenger seat without answering the call. He grabbed at the key in the ignition intending to start the car, when a thought struck him. They needed help. Just like Clay had needed help. The kind of help that only he could provide. Bullock smiled and his eyes lost focus as he turned over the possibilities in his mind.

Fifty Three

With a plan more or less worked out, DS Bullocks stopped at the first petrol station he came to. Sauntering into the shop and whistling like he didn't have a care in the world, he picked a bright red petrol can from the display shelves and took it over to the counter.

"Run out of petrol have you?" asked the boy behind the till. Or at least Bullock thought it was a boy. Who knew any more, when many of the teenagers wore androgynous clothes and both sexes wore make up.

"No, not me, I'd never do that. It's for the lawn mower."

The boy looked out of the window where storm clouds were gathering and it was clearly about to rain.

"The forecast is good for tomorrow," Bullock said.

"Whatever. You want any petrol with that?"

Bullock bit the inside of his cheek to stop him uttering the sarcastic comment that he'd have trouble using the petrol lawn mower without it, and simply nodded instead.

"Which pump?"

"Number two, five pounds of unleaded petrol."

Bullock was still cross with the bloody idiot behind

the till and so wasn't concentrating when he was filling the can and as a result splashed petrol over his shoes. Jerking the nozzle free of the can in disgust caused him to spray his brown suit with petrol. Irritated that he'd have to take it to the dry cleaners tomorrow, he looked down at the petrol stains that were spreading along his leather shoes and he realised he'd have to wear a dry pair of shoes as well as dry clothes, but couldn't remember if he had any black ones to go with his spare grey suit. With his worries about shoes and suits going round and round in his brain, he stowed the can in the boot and drove away, opening the windows so he wouldn't die from the petrol fumes that were filling the car, emanating from his shoes and clothes.

Despite the smell of petrol, he began to feel a bit peckish and he realised he hadn't really eaten properly since he'd turned on Enid, well killed Enid he supposed he should call it and noticing a McDonalds near to the petrol station, he drove around to the fast food outlet. Taking off his jacket and leaving it behind in the car, he walked in and queued up for food. He was thinking of the shock on Enid's face as she'd slithered, dead, to the floor and a manic giggle escaped him, causing the server to give him a strange look. Recognising that he needed to be more careful and couldn't afford to draw attention to himself, Bullock chose a table well away from anyone else and enjoyed his big mac and large fries, topped off with a chocolate milk shake, in peace. As he ate he looked out of the large plate glass windows and saw it was dark. He looked at his watch. 9pm. Excellent, they'd be going to bed soon.

Putting his discarded wrappings in the bin and his tray on the top of it, he left the McDonalds and returned to his car. Looking in the rear view mirror as he smoothed down his hair, he once again giggled with glee, but this time out loud as he was alone. Everything was great. Everything was going according to plan. Just this one last job and he'd be free. Free and clear. His mouth stretched in a grin and his eyes danced with delight.

***

A few hours later, the job was done and he was running across the grass in the back garden which was lit by the crackling flames. He slipped through the gate in the fence and walked to his car, which was parked in the shadows a little way down the road. He allowed himself a little skip in his step, feeling as happy as a child capering home after an arduous day at school. No one would be able to tell on him now. There was no one left to.

Sitting in the car and before he turned the key, he allowed himself a moment of reflected glory. How clever he'd been, he thought to himself. He'd silenced Enid, then Clay and now the old folk. He'd rid himself of anyone who could identify him, or tell on him. They were all dead, and that included the child who'd died of an overdose of ketamine.

His good mood lasted all the way home, where he made a cup of tea and then watched the 24 hour news channel whilst sipping it. It wasn't until he was showered and in bed that he realised what he'd forgotten. Or rather who he'd forgotten. Hope, or Bethany, or whatever the hell they called her. She was still alive and he still couldn't remember if she'd ever seen him without his hood on. He was fairly certain that she hadn't and smiled in satisfaction and turned over in bed, pulling the duvet up over his shoulders and spread out his legs, now that Enid was no longer in the way and taking up far more than her fair share of the bed.

No, he was safe. He was sure of it. Wasn't he?

Fifty Four

Crane hated house fires; he had ever since Sgt Barnes had died in one a few years back. It had taken a long time to get the sight of Barnes' body, twisted and burned to a crisp, with clawed hands and bent limbs, out of his mind. And here he was at the scene of another one, limping his way from the car behind Anderson towards the house. Luckily the fire was in a detached property, so there had been little chance of the fire spreading to the other houses in the street, but they had all been evacuated as a precaution. People were stood around in their night clothes in the early morning chill, pulling dressing gowns around their cold bodies, stamping feet and rubbing hands, their breath making eerie plumes of mist which hung around their heads in wisps as they spoke to each other.

As Crane and Anderson approached the front door of the burnt out house, Major Martin the local pathologist based at Frimley Park Hospital emerged, his protective white suit smudged black on the legs and arms from where he'd moved around the scene.

"Morning, Major," called Anderson.

"Oh, morning, Derek, Crane," the Major said as he

walked towards them, his large case bumping against his leg.

"What have we got?" asked Anderson, pulling out a handkerchief and holding it to his nose as the acrid smell of burnt wood, plastic and flesh reached them.

Crane pulled a jar of Vicks from his pocket and after swabbing his nostrils with the clear menthol smelling gel, offered the jar to Anderson.

"Two dead. Extensive damage to the house. The fire brigade are fairly certain an accelerant was used, probably petrol."

"Cause of death?" asked Crane.

"Really?" said the Major.

"Really," answered Crane.

"There's no way to tell until I get them on the table, as you well know."

Crane grinned in reply. He'd missed the banter with his old colleague and it felt good to be back in the harness again, pulling on his role like a well-worn but favourite suit. When a military detective, Crane had enjoyed working with Major Martin who, upon retirement from the Army, had transferred to Frimley Park Hospital in a civilian role.

"Any idea who they are?" asked Anderson from behind his hankie.

"The occupants of the house, sir," said DC Douglas as he approached them. "An elderly couple, one male, one female."

"Exactly," confirmed the Major. "Right, I'm off for a shower and change of clothes."

"Post mortem?" asked Crane.

"Jesus, did you really have to come back to work, Crane? Oh, all right 2pm sharp. And don't be late or I'll start without you," and with a rustle and bustle of self-importance, he waddled away.

"Douglas," Anderson said. "Any idea who the victims are?"

"Yes, sir," Douglas replied consulting his notebook. "Mr and Mrs Underwood, according to the next door neighbour."

"Who's that?" asked Crane.

"An older lady with rollers in her hair and wearing a pink dressing gown. There she is," Douglas pointed her out, "just going back into her house."

The crowd was beginning to disperse as the fire brigade had confirmed that there was no longer a danger to nearby properties and everyone was making their slow way home. It seemed they were lingering, as though not wishing the excitement over, despite the chill air.

"What's her name?"

"Olive Norman."

"Right, carry on interviewing the other residents, we'll take Mrs Norman. Come on, Crane," Anderson said.

Mrs Norman seemed tickled pink that detectives had come to interview her. Standing in her doorway she said, "I've just spoken to a very nice young man. Is he with you lot?"

"Indeed he is, Mrs Norman."

"You better come in then. Want tea?"

"No you're alright," said Crane, negotiating the step with the help of his walking stick.

"Sorry about the smell," she said as she led them into her living room. "I expect it's going to take ages to get it out of the house. Still," she said sitting in what clearly was her favourite armchair as next to it was a high table with a mug on it and yesterday's newspaper, "at least I'm alive, eh? Which is more than can be said for them next door," and she wiped a tear away from her eye.

"What can you tell us about your neighbours?" Anderson leaned forward, his elbows on his knees. Crane was sat next to Anderson's upright chair, but on a saggy settee that he wasn't sure how he was going to get up from.

"Nice couple, getting on a bit, you know? But they were lucky with their daughter."

"Lucky?"

"Yes, she moved into the area so she could be on hand to help them. I've no children myself, so I expect it will be an old people's home for me."

"Come now, Mrs Norman, that's many years away yet I'm sure."

"Let's hope so," and she shifted her gaze to look out of the window. "I'll miss my garden something rotten though."

"Um, to get back to next door?"

"Oh, yes, sorry, always here she was, morning noon and night."

"She was?"

"Yes, but thinking about it, I've not seen her for a few days now. Maybes a week. I did wonder where she was. I thought perhaps she was ill."

"What's her name, Mrs Norman?" Crane could feel that old prickle on his arms, as though the hairs on his skin were waking up and beginning to smell a clue.

"Her name? Only know her first name, Enid it is."

"When did she start coming on a regular basis?"

"Oh about three months ago I'd say. Her and her husband had just moved down from Birmingham….."

"Thank you, Mrs Norman," Anderson stood abruptly, signalling the end of the interview. "Someone will be in touch to take your statement, if that's alright?"

"Yes, yes, of course it is. Are you sure you have to go?

A cup of tea?"

"No, really, thank you all the same," and Anderson turned for the door as Crane was still struggling to get up. At last he managed it and hobbling after Anderson down the path said, "Are you thinking what I'm thinking?"

"Damn right I am," Anderson flung over his shoulder without slowing his stride. "Let's get back to the station."

Crane had just hobbled up to the car when Anderson's mobile rang.

"It's the office," said Anderson, answering the call and putting it on speaker.

"Guv, Holly here. Where are you?" the analyst's voice crackled out of the mobile.

"At the scene of the house fire. We're just leaving now and will be at the station in about 20 minutes."

"Um, you might want to do a detour, sir."

Anderson and Crane looked at each other across the roof of the car.

"Detour? What's happened now?" Anderson asked and Crane was unable to stop the sinking feeling inside. He'd left the house while it was still dark that morning and despite the smell of the house fire he was really looking forward to a coffee and something to eat for breakfast from the police station canteen. But it seemed the dead weren't finished with him and Anderson just yet.

"A dead body," she said, just as Crane feared.

"Jesus Christ, another one?" he blurted.

"Afraid so."

"Where's the body?" asked Anderson.

"Actually, it's more a matter of who, as well as where, sir."

"Go on, make my day," said Anderson but Crane

noted that his friend's sardonic smile didn't reach his eyes.

"From the description given by the uniforms first on the scene, it's that bloke we're looking for, the second one to get that sulphur tattoo. His body has been found at the tip in Ash, thrown away like a piece of rubbish. A couple of fly tippers went to dump some building rubble and they'd had a bit of a shock when one of them fancied a rolled up carpet they'd found there. When they opened it to check the condition, they'd found a body instead of a few holes."

"Where's DS Bullock?" Anderson asked.

"Here in the office, sir."

"Get him to meet us there would you?"

Fifty Five

Thrown away like a piece of rubbish, was about right, Crane decided as he and Anderson stood looking at the dead body of the man they'd been searching for. Just as Blake had told them, the tattoo of the sign of the sulphur was clearly visible on the man's shoulder. The other thing that was clearly visible, was a piece of wood, which seemed attached to his head with rusty nails.

"Is the Major on his way?" Crane asked looking towards the road in case he could see the Pathologist's car.

"Apparently so and he's none too happy about it, as he'd just arrived back at the mortuary when the call out came."

Crane looked at his watch and saw that it was already 11 am. "This probably means the post mortem of the couple from the fire will be delayed. Still, this one is fairly clear cut," said Crane turning to the body. "If the blow on the head hadn't killed him, septicaemia from the rusty nails probably would have," quipped Crane.

"Can you see, Bullock? Come over here, man. What's the matter with you?" Anderson asked his DS, who had just arrived and was hovering behind Crane.

"Nothing, guv, I've seen enough."

Crane thought Bullock's complexion had a bit of a green tinge to it as he turned to look at the man. "Don't you think it interesting there's not much blood on the carpet," Crane pointed to it and moved out of the way so that Bullock had a clear view of the tatty old rug. And of the body.

"Mm," Bullock mumbled, his hand covering his mouth, as though he were about to throw up.

"Killed somewhere else and then wrapped in the carpet and brought here," Anderson said. "Don't you think so, Bullock?"

"Mm," Bullock said again, and he took a few steps backwards.

"Are you feeling alright?" Crane asked him.

"Mm."

"Sure?"

But Bullock didn't reply, and as Crane and Anderson watched he turned and legged it for his car, where he steadied himself with a hand on the bonnet as he threw up.

"Must still be the effects of that dodgy prawn sandwich, don't you think?" Crane said.

"Either that or he's allergic to dead bodies."

"Allergic to work, more like," said Crane, not bothering to hide his disdain for the man.

"He's definitely a bit of a queer fish," said Anderson. "I can't make him out. He came from Birmingham with such good references."

Crane stilled. "He came from Birmingham, did you say?"

"Bloody hell. Yet another connection."

"First the dead couple with a daughter the same name as Bullock's wife and now we find he's connected to

Birmingham which is where the girls were taken from. They've got to be more than co-incidences, surely."

"I'd say so," agreed Anderson. "But we've got no proof."

"Not yet," said Crane watching Bullock chugging down some water as he leaned against his car.

Fifty Six

Crane wasn't sure why he was there. Surely the burnt and blackened corpses, that didn't really look like people anymore, couldn't tell them anything. He voiced that thought to Major Martin, his voice muffled by the mask he was wearing, which made the smell only slightly more bearable.

"You'd be surprised, Crane."

"Alright, I'm prepared to be surprised," but Crane's doubt could be heard in his voice, even through the mask.

He shifted slightly on the high stool on wheels that the Major's assistant had brought for him to sit on. Crane was pathetically grateful for this small kindness which had made a great deal of difference to his pain. But being a proud man he could only bring himself to grunt his thanks.

"No Anderson?" the Major asked. "I thought you two were joined at the hip."

"He's upstairs, having a meeting with Bethany and her parents. They wanted to talk about when she could go home."

"So you drew the short straw?"

"You could put it like that, but to be fair people skills aren't the top of my list of 'things that I'm best at'."

"Don't I know it," and the Major's eyes, which were the only part of his face that Crane could see, crinkled in amusement, alluding to previous cases they'd worked on together when Crane was Sgt Major Crane, in charge of the Special Investigations Branch of the Military Police Unit based at Aldershot Garrison. Crane had long ago lost count of the cases they'd both been involved in.

All through the conversation, the Major had been cutting and slicing, placing specimens in jars and on slides. His hands moved so fast at times that Crane alluded to him as being the second Edward Scissor Hands. Then they stilled.

"What is it?" Crane scooted closer to the body.

"They were alive."

"What? When the fire started?"

"Yes. See, there's burning in the oesophagus. They'd inhaled the scorching air."

"Both of them?"

"I've only done the male, but I expect it will be same in the female."

"How do you know this is a male?" Crane indicated the burned blob of what could have been mistaken for a particularly large piece of coal or charcoal.

"Not from any genitals, that's for sure."

That's what Crane had thought.

"It's the size and shape of the pelvis. The clothes and most of the flesh may have been burned away, but underneath the skeleton is remarkably well preserved. Which takes me to my second point."

Crane got the impression he wasn't going to like the second point any more than he'd liked the first.

"Some of the burns on the body show evidence of

burning at a different temperature than the others."

"Sorry?"

"In a fierce fire the clothes or bedclothes melt into the flesh, but at a lower, more normal temperature for a fire the body burns in layers; the clothes are burned away first, then the skin, then the fat…"

"I get it, no more description necessary, thanks."

"Oh, I was just getting started."

Crane said, "Well stop and tell me what this flash burning means."

The Major laid down his scalpel and looked at Crane. "They were doused in petrol in their bed. When I was at the scene I was chatting to the Fire Officer, who told me they'd found evidence of a trail of accelerant, most probably petrol, running from the back door, up the stairs and into the bedroom."

"So the house and the old couple were deliberately set alight."

The Major nodded and turned back to the body once more, but Crane had seen enough and heard enough. He needed to go and tell Anderson that they were not only looking for a cold blooded killer, but a sadistic one at that.

"Thanks, Major, I'll be off now. You'll send your report through as soon as you can?"

"Sure. But I'll wait until I've done the post mortem on Mrs Underwood and then send them both through together."

"Of course."

Crane grabbed his stick, nodded to the Major's assistant and left the morgue, his brain grappling with what he'd just been told. Who could have had such a hatred of Mr and Mrs Underwood that they could have done something like that? Surely Bullock wasn't that type of man? If it was Bullock? He was a policeman. A champion of the law, But if their theory proved correct and Bullock's wife Enid was the Underwood's daughter, then Bullock had killed his parents-in-law, in one of the most horrible ways imaginable. The thought made Crane shiver, despite the warmth of the hospital corridors.

Fifty Seven

Crane and Anderson wound their way through the incident room, their destination being the relative quiet of Anderson's office. They were worn down. Exhausted by a day in which they'd witnessed three bodies before lunch-time. Even by Crane's reckoning this was the worst day he'd ever had as an investigator. He never wanted to see a burnt body again, nor a dead man that had a piece of wood lodged in his skull.

The whole thing was beyond him. There was a maniac on the loose and they didn't know who it was. Who would he go after next? Would he turn on members of the team, the closer they got to finding him and the more he panicked? For that's what Crane thought was happening. Their killer, whoever he or she may be, seemed to be seeing people as a threat and then eliminating them. So there must be a connection between Mr and Mrs Underwood and Clay. Crane just didn't know what it was yet. It was inconceivable that there were two killers abroad in Aldershot at the same time.

Crane seemed to wade through the warm air of the large open space where the rest of the detectives, analysts and civilian employees worked. The air was fetid; a soupy mixture of sweat, stale food and stale cigarettes, all emanating from the clothes the team were wearing. A mirage of the steam lifting from each person made Crane stumble and to stop himself from falling he had to grab the corner of a desk.

"Douglas," Anderson barked. "Help Crane into the office and then go and fetch us two cups of tea."

Douglas sprang from his desk and grabbed Crane's arm.

"I'm alright," Crane said, shaking his arm to try and dislodge Douglas' hand.

Anderson said, "No you're not, Crane. I know that because I'm not. So shut up and accept help for once."

Crane did as he was told, too exhausted to be angry with his friend. Douglas led him to Anderson's office and Crane had to admit that it felt good to lean on a fit young man, taking the pressure off his hip. Crane could remember when he had been young and fit himself and wondered where the years had gone.

After depositing Crane in a chair in Anderson's office, Douglas said, "Guv, I've…"

"Got to go and get the tea," snapped Anderson, settling in the chair behind his desk.

"But…"

"Two sugars," gasped Crane and rummaged in his pocket for his pain killers, "and a glass of water so I can take these."

"Yes, guv, I'll be right back," said DC Douglas as he scurried away.

"I take it you're shattered and fed up too," Crane lifted his head to look at Anderson.

"Yes and the fact that I can't make head nor tail out of the whole sorry mess is just making it worse, because I'm adding worry to the exhaustion."

"That's pretty much where I'm at. So it's time to do something about it."

"What? Everyone out there is working their arses off, Crane. We can't fault them for that."

"I know, Derek, I'm not saying anyone is at fault, I'm just saying that perhaps we need to look at the case, or cases, from another angle."

"What bloody angle?"

"Connections."

Just then Douglas appeared in the doorway, holding a tray of drinks.

"Douglas, go and get a white board marker and a cloth would you?"

"Um, yes, Crane, but…"

"But nothing."

"No, of course not," and Douglas left the office again.

By the time Crane had taken his tablets, Douglas was back. "Right, clean that board would you? We're going to explore connections. I used to do this at the Garrison, only then I could stand upright for more than a few minutes at a time, so you'll have to write for me, Douglas. But first close the door and drop the blinds. We don't want this to become general knowledge."

"What are we doing, Crane? I'm too knackered to think," grumbled Anderson.

"A mind map, Derek. Right, Douglas, write up on the board randomly the following names: Bethany, Dawn, Mr and Mrs Underwood and Clay with plenty of space between them. Oh, put up Satanic Church and Enid as well and a question mark for our unidentified killer. On second thoughts, put the killer in the middle of the names."

As Douglas wrote, Crane sipped his tea. "Any biscuits, Derek?"

"No, you've eaten them all."

"Ah, sorry. I'll bring in some more tomorrow then. Right," Crane turned to the board. "Bethany. Draw a connecting line from Bethany to the Satanic Church and one to Dawn as both girls were found with Satanic symbols on their arms. And of course a link from Dawn to the Satanic Church."

"Then, we need an ice cream van on there as well and both girls connected to it," said Derek.

"Mr and Mrs Underwood need connecting to their daughter Enid and to the killer.

"Clay…"

"Sir, about Clay."

"Yes?"

"Um, his finger prints match the ones taken from the ice cream van."

"What?"

"Why didn't you tell us this before," spluttered Anderson. "That's vital information, Douglas."

"I know, sir, I've been trying to tell you, but I had to get the teas, then clean the board, then…"

"Alright, that'll do." Crane thought that Anderson was as angry with himself as he was with his young DC, indicated by the way a slight flush had spread across the DI's cheeks. "Is there anything else we should know?"

"Yes, sir. There were a couple of ginger hairs found on the body. With the roots still on."

Fifty Eight

"Douglas, leave the room."

"Guv?"

"Didn't you hear me?"

"Um, right."

As Douglas moved towards the door, Anderson added, "And shut the door behind you and this meeting never took place. Understand?"

"Understood, sir," Douglas agreed, even though his eyes were full of unanswered questions.

"And if DS Bullock asks what's going on, you've just been getting us tea and biscuits."

"Oh, I see."

"And the blinds are closed because Crane's not feeling too good what with his hip and all."

"Exactly, sir," Douglas at last seemed to get the hang of the conversation as he nodded emphatically.

Once Douglas had backed out of the door and closed it behind him, Crane said, "Wasn't that a bit of an overreaction?"

"No. Douglas is a good lad, but he works opposite Bullock and reports to him."

"And you want Bullock as far away as possible."

"Right." Anderson struggled out of his chair and picked up the whiteboard pen. "Let's get on with it."

By the time they'd finished they were both beyond exhaustion, but felt confident they'd got all the links.

Bethany and Dawn were linked to each other, to the ice cream van that was used to abduct them, to Birmingham where they'd lived, to the Satanic Church via the symbols on their arms and the bloodletting, to the sign of the sulphur also on their arms and through that to the tattoos, and of course to Clay, who had, at the very least, abducted them.

Clay was linked to the girls, the ice cream van, the Church, the tattoos, Birmingham and to the person who killed him who had ginger hair.

Mr and Mrs Underwood were linked to their daughter, Enid and to Birmingham where she'd come from and to their killer, of course.

Enid was linked to Birmingham, her dead parents Mr and Mrs Underwood and her husband, who happened to be DS Bullock, who just happened to have ginger hair.

The tattoo shop was linked to Clay and possibly to their killer, who had had a sulphur tattoo done as well and had been described as having ginger hair.

If their killer was who they thought he was, he was linked to the Satanic Church via the tattoos and therefore via the Church to the abducted girls and through them to Clay and Birmingham. But he could also be connected to Clay as his killer. And to Birmingham because that's where he came from. And to Enid as she was his wife. And to the Underwoods as he was their son-in-law.

"Are we any further forward?" asked Crane.

Anderson nodded. He was secretly pleased with Crane's idea that had helped clarify the muddle of clues and shown how the people involved related to each other, but he had no intention of telling him so. They were a team now, so in order to be able to work closely with each other, neither should have the upper hand, or the bigger ego. And as Crane's ego was a pretty fragile thing, Anderson didn't want to mention anything that could, instead of pleasing him, remind him of the man he used to be, thereby plunging him into the cloud of depression that, whilst mostly being kept at bay, still hovered close by.

Anderson went and peeked through the blind which was covering the glass panel in the wall of his office and that overlooked the general area. Satisfied with what he saw he picked up the phone on his desk. "Douglas," he said as the phone was answered.

"Yes, guv?"

"The office is looking a right mess. Gather up the empty mugs from the desks would you?"

"Oh, right, guv." DS Douglas could be seen through the glass panel looking around at the pristine office as the cleaners had already been round. The only two mugs on view were his own and the one on the desk opposite him.

"Oh, and you might want to wear gloves because your hands might get in a mess. And pick up DS Bullock's mug first would you? And put it in a clean plastic bag for protection. You wouldn't want to break it."

Douglas did as he was told and entered Anderson's office, mug in hand in a plastic evidence bag. "I take it this hasn't happened either, guv?" he grinned.

"Absolutely right," confirmed Anderson. "Time to go home, I think."

Fifty Nine

The following morning Anderson was up and about early, going to Frimley Park Hospital to see Bethany, but leaving Crane at home for a bit of a lie-in. Last night he'd gone home via the Crime Lab, where he'd dropped off Bullock's mug and given specific instructions as to its testing and then comparison of the results. Although he'd been at dropping point, he'd been aware of the problems that could have occurred with the chain of evidence, if he'd taken it home with him and then dropped it off the following morning. If they were to get the result they wanted in the case, every piece of evidence had to be allowable in court and without any possibility of it being contaminated. He couldn't, for instance, have left it in his car overnight without being challenged about it. Equally as bad would have been to leave it in his house, amid the chaos of his family life. So even though he'd been on the point of collapse himself, never mind Crane, it had been better to be safe than sorry and run that one last errand.

Anderson made his solitary way up to Bethany's room. After fielding the usual questions from her parents as to when she could travel back to Birmingham with them, he called for the FLO to act as a witness and then showed Bethany a parade of six photographs, all men of similar looks.

"Do you see the picture of the man who took you?" he asked the wan child. He hoped she would put some weight on soon; it was upsetting to see her still so pale and thin. The health professionals seemed to think she'd start eating soon. In the meantime they were trying to entice her with nutrient drinks. Apparently, the chocolate one was proving a bit of a hit.

Bethany nodded in answer to Anderson's question.

"Can you point to him?"

Raising a shaking arm, Bethany managed to place her finger on Clay's picture, but immediately withdrew it and began to cry. As her sobs increased in force and in volume, Anderson made way for her mother who had rushed into the room as the sounds of her daughter's distress carried out into the corridor.

"What have you done to her?" she snapped, taking both Anderson and the FLO in with her sweeping gaze.

"We had to show her some pictures," the FLO explained. "She managed to point out her abductor, which is a great help to us."

"But it upset her beyond reason," hissed her mother. "Get out, both of you and leave her alone."

Anderson and the FLO retreated.

"Sorry, the wife's a bit protective at the moment," Bethany's father said as they joined him outside the room.

"That's understandable, I'm sorry but we had to…"

"I know. But its best you push off now."

Anderson agreed and went to turn away.

"Mr Anderson?"

"Yes?" Anderson turned back.

"Is she safe? Or do you think the bastard who did this to her will come for her?"

"Honestly?"

"Of course."

"I really don't know. We've found her abductor. He is dead, so that's that. But we haven't found another man that we're looking for, who we believe to be behind the abductions. So it's better to err on the side of caution and leave someone with her at all times. When you and your wife go for a break, the FLO and another police officer will stay here. It's not worth taking any chances is it?"

"Thanks," Bethany's father nodded and smiled though his eyes shone with tears of sorrow, not happiness. As he turned away Derek wondered if and when the family would ever feel truly safe and happy again.

***

Anderson hoped that it was a much refreshed Crane that he was to pick up from his home in Ash. It was midmorning by the time he arrived, which had given Crane a bit of extra sleep and a slower start to his day.

"How are you today?" Anderson asked, once Crane was settled in the passenger seat.

"Great."

Anderson looked closely at his friend and saw, despite Crane's clean suit and crisp white shirt, the strain on his face, the wince of pain as he got in the car and the dark shadows under his eyes. "Try again."

"Fucking awful. There, is that better?"

"It's nearer the truth at any rate."

"Anyway enough of me, did you drop off the mug?"

"Yes, last night," said Anderson starting the car.

"And how was Bethany today?"

"Pretty much like you," said Anderson and explained what had happened.

"Good work, though," said Crane. "It's a good thing that she picked out Clay's photo, kind of closes the circle on that one."

"Not that he'll ever be brought to justice now."

Crane said, "No, but him being dead and all is a kind of justice in itself."

"But with him out of the picture, we don't know who's behind all this."

"Behind the Satanic Church, you mean?"

"Yeah, if there is a Church at all."

"Of course there is, Derek," said Crane. "Have faith," and a lopsided grin split his face, chasing away some of the pain etched there.

Sixty

Crane had been eagerly awaiting this particular trip out since they'd agreed on it last night. His buoyant mood and just plain out and out exhaustion had helped chase some of the demons away last night and the rest had done his body good. The pain wasn't gone, though, and Crane doubted it ever would. His other problem was the fact that he'd been sitting down too much over the past few days and hadn't had time to do the exercises the physiotherapist had insisted he do. At the time Crane had thought they were nothing more than a nuisance, but was becoming to realise the importance of keeping his hip and leg moving as much as possible and he vowed to keep up with the exercises every day in future, although at the moment he had no idea when he was going to fit them into his busy schedule. Perhaps he'd start a new regime once this case was over.

That thought, of course, led him to think about the future. It was all very well being employed as a civilian expert for this case, but what would happen once it finished? Doubts clouded his eyes and his brow furrowed as he looked into the deep rabbit hole he was teetering on the edge of, and the dark thoughts were threatening to dispel his good mood and tip him over the edge into the abyss.

"Crane? You alright?" Anderson's voice pierced the depression clouding Crane's view of the world.

"Sorry?"

"Focus please. This is no ordinary visit we're about to embark on."

"No," Crane adjusted his position in the car seat, but it didn't appease the gremlins who were attacking his hip joint with newer, sharper knives. "You're right. Sorry."

Anderson was quiet for a moment whilst he navigated the latest roundabout in the road.

"Does anyone know where we are this morning?" asked Crane.

"Only Holly. She gave me the details on Bullock that I wanted this morning."

"Don't you already have those, as his direct boss?"

"Personnel files aren't held in offices anymore. They're all on the computer - somewhere."

"Somewhere?"

"Yeah, and I can never remember where that somewhere is, so Holly got them for me."

Crane snorted with laughter as Anderson pulled up in front of a semi-detached house in a quiet residential street in Farnborough. They sat in the car for a moment looking at the 1970's façade, the pebbledash exterior and the empty driveway.

Anderson said, "No car on the driveway."

"Could be in the garage."

"Maybe. There's only one way to find out. Come on."

They walked up the drive in the eerily quiet street. There was no one walking a dog, pushing a pram, or even taking a solitary stroll.

Crane said, "It's very quiet here," as he looked

around. "It's spooky."

"Get a grip, Crane. It's not Wayward Pines."

"Wayward Pines?"

"Cult TV series."

"You need to get a life, Derek."

"Ha, looks who's talking."

They arrived at Bullock's front door and Anderson rang the doorbell. Getting no reply, he rang again and then a third time, but there was still no answer and no movement could be seen inside the house through the large picture windows.

Crane said, "Let's try next door."

Instead of cutting across the grass they politely walked back down the path and then up to the house next door. This time their ring was answered so quickly that Crane thought the neighbour must have been standing behind the door waiting for them.

"Good morning," Anderson said to the large woman who stood there, wiping her hands on an apron tied around her ample waist. "We were hoping to speak to Mrs Bullock, next door, but there's no sign of her."

"Who are you?"

Anderson made the introductions and the woman's eyes brightened with curiosity.

"Have you seen Mrs Bullock lately?" he asked.

"Enid? No, no I haven't. Bit strange that."

"Strange? Why?" Crane asked.

"Because she's always in and out of the house, popping over to her parents, shopping and stuff. Gets quiet annoying, her car backwards and forwards every day."

"But not lately?"

"No. Not seen or heard of her for a few days now. Only seen him. Is she alright?"

Anderson ignored her question and asked, "What type of car does she have?"

"Well, I'm not normally good with cars, but hers is easy, one of those new Mini things. Bright red, difficult to miss."

"And the roof?"

"Eh?"

"The roofs are normally a different colour on a mini."

"Oh, right, a Union Jack. Very patriotic I always thought. Is she alright?"

But the neighbour didn't look concerned for Enid's welfare, only interest in the mystery and Crane wondered how long it would take for the gossip mill to start grinding. A few seconds after they left was his expectation.

"Where is it normally parked?"

"In the garage over night, but it's normally on the drive during the day."

Anderson said, "Thank you, you've been very helpful," and nodding to Crane turned away from the door.

"Is that it?" the woman called after them. "Don't I have to make a statement? The name is Mrs Ball, just in case you need me again!"

"Back to the station?" asked Crane.

"In a minute, first I want to check the garage, come on."

They followed the stepping stone path down the side of Bullock's house, where they found a back door into the garage. They didn't need to open it, as a red Mini with a Union Jack roof could be clearly seen through the glass panel.

"Enid's maiden name is Underwood," said Anderson and Crane had to hold onto the garage wall with one hand and his stick with the other, to stop himself falling over.

Sixty One

DS Bullock was sweating so much he could feel the damp patches under his arms cold and clammy against his skin. The collar around his neck seemed to be strangling him and he loosened his tie and undid the top button of his shirt, gulping in great lungs full of air, which only served to make his head reel. He had no idea how he'd managed to get through the day yesterday, after being called out by Anderson to the dead body at the tip.

He'd met Crane and Anderson there, doing and saying as little as possible, standing as far away from the body as he could get and literally hiding behind his notebook as he took down Anderson's instructions. He didn't volunteer any opinion, as to be honest he was pretty much incapable of speech. It was as if he had disassociated, watching himself and the other two policemen from a distance. It had felt very unreal. He only hoped that he'd managed to pull it off and that Anderson and Crane hadn't noticed anything out of the ordinary. Luckily he wasn't normally the chattiest of people, so he reckoned he was alright.

He'd been plagued by visions in his sleep all last night: fires, bodies burning to a crisp and the smell of acrid smoke sharp in the bedroom; images of his dead wife so real that he was convinced he'd heard her snoring in the wee small hours. To top it all, he'd just had to endure the morning meeting. Faced with large pictures of Clay blown up on the screen, he'd nearly thrown up again. Somehow it made what he'd done more real than when he'd been at the rubbish tip. It was seeing the nails buried into Clay's skull and the look of surprise frozen forever on his face, he supposed. Before, killing him had seemed like something he'd done in a dream. He wasn't really there at the time, not in his head that was. In his head he was just doing what he had to do to save himself. To free himself. To make sure that everything would come alright in the end.

A couple of people had already asked if he was feeling alright and he'd just mumbled something intelligible in reply before barging his way back to his desk. All he wanted was to be left alone, left in peace, to carry on his work in the Satanic Church. The room started to roll under his feet as he tried to think about what to do next. But he couldn't think in the office, he had to get away.

"You alright?" he heard DC Douglas ask. Even though Douglas was sitting opposite him, to Bullock his voice seemed to come from a long way away with an accompanying echo and he shook his head to try and clear his ears.

"What's wrong?"

"Dunno," Bullock said, putting his hands up to his head in an effort to stop the dizzy spell. "Think I've got a migraine." Struggling out of his chair and then clutching the desk for support he said, "I've got to go home."

"But we're short-handed, what with the fires and all these bodies," said Douglas.

"I know but I can't think, I can't see, I've got distorted vision. I've got to get out of here."

Bullock lurched away, nearly falling over a rubbish bin and just about managing to right himself.

"Oh for God's sake go home then," shouted Douglas, "and take a taxi."

Bullock lifted his arm in acknowledgement as he half-fell, half-walked through the CID office door, out into the corridor and followed the scent of the freedom that he hoped was just within his grasp.

Sixty Two

As Crane and Anderson got back into to their car Anderson was already on the phone.

"Douglas, where's DS Bullock?"

"On his way home, guv, he says he has a bad migraine."

"Migraine?"

"Well, whatever it is he looked bloody awful. I told him to get a taxi because as his vision was funny he could have an accident."

"When did he leave?"

"I'm not sure, but he's been gone a while now."

"Well he's not at home. We're here and he's not."

"Sorry, guv, no idea. Perhaps he couldn't find a taxi."

"Alright, thanks, Douglas," and Anderson closed the call.

"So," said Crane. "Do you want to wait here for him?"

"And say what? We think something's happened to your wife? No, I don't want to alert him to the fact that we're checking up on him. Let's go back to the station and plot our next move."

Anderson had just turned the car around to return to

Aldershot, when his phone rang again. So he tossed it to Crane who answered it and put it on speaker.

"Guv," said Douglas. "I've just had word from the hospital. Bethany has had a screaming fit. Something's happened."

"Christ! Is she okay?" Anderson screeched to a halt by the side of the road, the car rocking from the ferocity of his use of the brakes.

"They think so, but they've had to give her a mild sedative."

"Where was the FLO?" Anderson snapped.

"Had to go to the toilet, sir, but she thought it would be alright as, um, as…"

"What is it, Douglas?" Crane said.

"Um, it seems DS Bullock didn't go home. He was there at the hospital and he'd said he'd relieve the FLO, while she relieved herself."

"Those exact words?"

"Afraid so, sir. He also said she could pop downstairs to the café and get herself a decent coffee and a cake or something."

"And after that, that's when Bethany started to scream?"

"Yes, the nurse who was first in the room said she saw DS Bullock, um, he was, um, looming over Bethany with a pillow in his hands."

"Jesus Christ." Anderson closed his eyes.

"Is she sure?" asked Crane.

"Positive, sir. I can't quite believe it myself. What do you think it means?"

But Crane didn't reply as Anderson was already turning the car around, yet again, this time pointing it in the direction of Frimley Park Hospital.

"Put out an APB on DS Bullock and his car. Give his

registration number to all patrol cars, we need to find him – now!" said Crane on Anderson's behalf, as his friend's sole focus seemed to be the road ahead and his grip on the steering wheel.

Sixty Three

Bullock was having a bad day. A very bad day. After his melt down in the office, well panic attack he supposed it was, his vision had returned to normal once he was out in the fresh air. He'd paused for a moment in the car park and bending over he'd placed his hands on his thighs and taken deep breaths. As his heart rate slowed and became a steady beat rather than a mad jazzy syncopated one, his thoughts had cleared, enabling him to plot his next move. And that simple action, that decision, had helped to calm him, to ground him. The plan he'd decided on was that he'd have to go to the hospital and see Bethany. Only then would he be able to answer the question; had she ever seen him without his hood on? As he'd finally had a purpose, he'd been able to lift his head from his knees and walk to his car, deciding that sod taking a taxi, he was capable of driving.

Upon his arrival at the hospital, he'd found that Bethany's parents had gone back to their hotel for a shower and change of clothes and that the only person in attendance was the FLO, Victoria Fleming. Seeing Bullock through the windows, she'd come outside.

Offering to give her a break, he'd shooed her off in the direction of the cafeteria. The conversation had taken place outside Bethany's room, so Bullock still hadn't had the answer to his question. He knew he'd have to face his worst fears and so he'd grabbed the door knob and slowly turned it.

If she hadn't have recognised him, everything would have been fine, but she had. So he knew he'd have to shut her up. But that had been his problem. He hadn't had a chance to shut her up. She'd started screaming and he hadn't seen that she'd had the call button in her hand, so the screaming and the buzzer alerted the hospital staff much faster than he'd anticipated. All he'd managed to do was to back out of the room and run like hell. Luckily everyone was more concerned with Bethany than him, so he'd managed to get away.

But now he was sweating again and couldn't think what to do. He nearly ran over a pedestrian who'd started to cross the road on a zebra crossing and he cursed the man for being so stupid. He missed the corner turning left and mounted the kerb, causing all sorts of strange grinding noises to come from the underneath of the car. He knew he needed to calm down. Needed to find a safe place to go. And then he had it. The farm. No one had found that yet and that could be his bolt hole, his place of safety. He would go to ground and plan his long term escape. But first he needed some supplies. He had to have a cup of tea while he thought.

Sixty Four

Crane couldn't believe what he'd just seen. "There he is!" he shouted and pointed in the direction their car was already travelling.

"Where?" shouted Anderson, head going from side to side as he scanned the road for DS Bullock.

"Just coming out of the co-op supermarket on the left side of the road. What the bloody hell is he doing? He's never been shopping!" Crane could see a plastic carrier bag in Bullock's left hand. "Oh, now he's getting in his car. Fuck, he's seen us!" and Crane ducked below the windscreen, then realising what he'd done, sheepishly raised his head again. "Guess that doesn't matter, does it?"

"No," said Anderson, "it doesn't."

In front of them, DC Bullock's car pulled out onto the road and a puff of smoke burst from the car's exhaust pipe as he floored the accelerator of the Lexus, easily pulling away from Anderson's Ford. But Anderson wasn't to be outdone and rapidly changing down in gears, he viciously jabbed at his own accelerator pedal, taking the car to the maximum revs every time before changing up the gearbox.

As they were thrown from side to side Crane said, "Fucking hell, Derek, mind me, I don't want the other leg and hip broken."

Crane grabbed at the hand hold mounted near the roof of the car, on his left hand side, desperately trying to keep himself upright.

"Trust me, Crane," Anderson said. "I've done the course."

"What course?"

"Advanced driving."

"When?"

"Oh a few years back, well quite a few years actually."

"I can tell," gasped Crane, but he could see that Anderson was gaining on the bigger car, which was now filling the view from their windscreen. "How are you going to get him to stop?"

Anderson's reply was to hit the back of Bullock's car. The surprise move caused Bullock to brake, allowing Anderson to pull up level with the back wing of the Lexus. Pulling hard to the left on the steering wheel, Anderson hit the rear wing of the Lexus, pushing the back of the car to the left, sending the Lexus into a spin.

"Like that," Anderson shouted, momentarily deafening Crane in one ear.

But the manoeuvre had worked and the Lexus lurched to a stop sideways across the road. Anderson clambered out of his own car and ran to the Lexus as Crane grabbed the radio to call it in, watching with satisfaction as Anderson pulled Bullock from his vehicle and slapped a pair of hand cuffs around his wrists.

Sixty Five

Even though Crane had called the arrest in, which had alerted the team to what had happened, everyone still stopped what they were doing and turned to watch DS Bullock being escorted through the CID office to an interview room. As Crane limped alongside Anderson, he got a good look at their faces. The team were by turn incredulous, nervous and embarrassed by the arrest of one of their own. DC Douglas plopped down on his chair as his superior officer was pushed into the room, as though his legs suddenly wouldn't support him anymore, clearly unable to believe his eyes.

"Douglas, fetch us some teas, would you?"

"Um," Douglas mumbled, then catching sight of Crane's grim face, rapidly nodded his head and disappeared in the direction of the kitchen.

The three men sat down in the bland beige interview room with Crane and Anderson taking up their positions on the other side of the table, opposite Bullock. Crane was just glad to sit on something that wasn't rocking and rolling around and as Douglas came in with the cups of tea, he shook a pain killer into his palm from a packet in his pocket and swallowed it with a sip of the hot liquid, not caring about the acrid taste of the melting pill.

Looking over at Bullock he saw a previously proud man who was now a shadow of his former self. His clothes were dishevelled, his hair all over the place, his eyes haunted and a five o'clock shadow adorned his cheeks and chin, although it was only mid-morning. The ginger hairs pushed through skin that was sallow and moulded his face into deep shadows under his now prominent cheek bones. Crane pushed a drink towards Bullock, who reached for it, unable to disguise the trembling of his hand as he raised it to his lips. After he'd taken a mouthful, Bullock returned the cup to the table and put his head in his hands.

"It seems you have a few problems at the moment, DS Bullock," Anderson said. "We'd like to talk to you about the abduction of two girls, the murder of one of them and the attempted murder of the other, the murder of Clay and of Mr and Mrs Underwood. Oh, and while we're at it, where's Enid?"

Bullock didn't answer, just took another drink of his tea.

"Is this how you're going to play it? Giving me the silent treatment?"

Still Bullock refused to answer, turning his head away from Anderson's questions.

"I rather think," said Crane, "that since you arrived in Aldershot from Birmingham, your whole life has begun to unravel."

Bullock closed his eyes.

"Correct me if I'm wrong, but your domestic situation mustn't have been that happy, what with Enid at her parent's house most of the time. Did that bother you, Bullock? That she had more time for them, than she'd ever had for you?"

"And how on earth did you get mixed up with Clay?" Anderson took up the questioning. "An idiotic petty criminal who couldn't even cover his tracks. Tracks that led us straight to you."

"I bet you wished you'd never seen Aldershot, or even heard of it, don't you Bullock?" said Crane.

"You'd have been much happier staying in Birmingham, I bet," added Anderson.

Crane noticed that Bullock's face was working; his eyes blinking rapidly and his jaw moving as though he were his name-sake masticating on grass. Underneath the table, his heel started bouncing up and down. But then he stilled.

"I want a lawyer or a Police Federation Rep," Bullock stated.

"Of course, that's your right," said Anderson. "But I thought we were just having a nice chat, colleague to colleague, you know?"

"I'm not bloody stupid, Anderson, although you always act as though I am. I know how this works. I want my phone call."

"Oh, to call Enid?" Crane asked all innocence.

Bullock stared at Crane, who for a fleeting moment had a glimpse of something dark and terrible in Bullock's eyes.

"To call my lawyer," Bullock reiterated.

Scraping their chairs across the floor as they stood, Crane and Anderson left the room without another word.

Outside in the corridor, Anderson asked Crane, "What do you think of him? Has he done all the things we suspect he has?"

Recalling the look in Bullock's eyes, Crane said, "He's capable of it, I've no doubt about that."

Anderson nodded and said, "I'll get a search warrant application drawn up for Bullock's house. Let's see what we find there and I'll include his car and Enid's car."

"Will you have trouble getting it?"

"What, as Bullock's a police officer you mean? Nah, I know just the judge for this one. Look, why don't you go home for a rest while we're waiting for the warrant and I'll swing round and pick you up on the way to Bullock's house."

"What about interviewing him again?"

"Nothing doing on that score. It'll take ages for a solicitor or a Federation Rep to arrive and then he'll have to have a private meeting with his client and I'd rather start the search before we speak to him again anyway. Go on with you and I'll make sure you don't miss anything."

"Promise?"

"Fuck off, Crane," Anderson said grinning. "I'll see you later."

As Crane hobbled his way out of the station towards the waiting car Anderson had arranged for him, he turned to look at the imposing but ugly grey granite building he'd just come out of. It didn't really matter if he worked for the police, or the army, he realised. Either way he was catching bad guys, which was what he was good at and loved to do. Especially catching men like Bullock. The look of pure evil he'd glimpsed in the man's eyes earlier still had the power to send a shiver down his spine.

Sixty Six

Upon Crane and Anderson's arrival at Bullock's house, Anderson nodded to the team waiting on the driveway, giving the signal for them to enter the house. Anderson had collected Bullock's keys on the way out of the station. He hadn't refused to give them to Anderson who had a legitimate search warrant, as it saved damage to his house and car. Bullock was still stewing on his own in the interview room, his solicitor apparently busy elsewhere, but promising to get to the police station as soon as he could. Anderson didn't know what was delaying the man, but the fact that he was being asked to represent a potentially bent copper maybe had something to do with it. Either way, Bullock didn't seem impressed and was looking more and more like a pressure cooker about to blow. Not wanting to place Bullock in the cells, Anderson had left him in a locked interview room with a policeman posted at the door for good measure.

As the forensic team swept into the house and fanned out, Crane and Anderson stood in the hallway for a moment, plastic suited with latex gloves on their hands and paper bootees over their shoes.

"I think it was a bit much having to wrap a paper bootee over my stick," grumbled Crane. "I look like a right dick."

"Procedure, Crane. I don't want to give Bullock's brief or Federation rep any cause for throwing out evidence that could have potentially been brought in on your stick. Anyway you could have left it in the car."

"Hmm, maybe next time," said Crane increasing the pressure on his stick slightly. He was beginning to wonder if his reliance on it was becoming more mental than physical, but pushed the thought away for consideration another day. When he wasn't in as much pain. When he wasn't so busy. When he wasn't so tired. When…

"Up here, guv. Found his office."

"Out here, boss," called another officer. "Got something in the garden."

Looking at the stairs, then back at his friend, Anderson said, "I'll go up, you go outside."

Relieved, Crane did as he was ordered and met a Forensic Officer outside on the patio who pushed his hood off his head and his mask off his face at Crane's approach, to reveal a young woman, startling Crane who had been expecting a man. "It's alright, sir," she grinned at the look on Crane's face. "I get that reaction a lot. These suits make us look pretty androgynous."

"No offence, meant," said Crane, being chivalrous for once.

"None taken. Just wanted to show you this, sir," and she pointed to a garden spade and fork, propped up against the wall of the house. Both were covered in muddy soil. There were tracks in the grass leading to a freshly turned flower bed up against the far fence.

"Shit," breathed Crane. Taking a few steps to the end

of the patio, he looked carefully at the grass without stepping on it. "Looks like there are two sets of tracks," he said. "One ridged as though he'd dragged the fork behind him as he walked and one flatter and broader as though he'd dragged something else. The spade maybe?"

"Don't think so, sir, the depressed grass is much wider than the spade in places and also I'd say that whatever it was it was a lot heavier than a spade."

"Enid."

"Sir? My name's Frankie."

"Enid is DS Bullocks' wife's name."

"Oh, I see."

"Unfortunately, so do I. Thanks, Frankie, I'll let DI Anderson know. That'll be all for now. Carry on."

It was only when Frankie gave him a strange look, did Crane realise he'd slipped back into army speak.. Flame-faced, he mumbled an apology and turned away, going back into the house to find Anderson. They met at the bottom of the stairs.

"I think we've found Enid," Crane said.

"And I think we've found the place where the girls were held. But you first."

Crane explained about the findings in the garden, but left out the part about his chauvinist gaff of expecting a man rather than a woman, and then the one where he'd addressed her as if she were one of his soldiers.

"I was afraid we might find Enid buried in the garden," said Anderson and Crane agreed with him.

"So, what have you got?"

Anderson said, "A farmhouse, in the countryside, in Enid's name."

Sixty Seven

Crane and Anderson, once more dressed in crime scene suits, stood silently staring at the farmhouse before them. Decrepit and aging, the house seemed to sag on its foundations, the drunken walls bowing out under the weight of the roof. The roof itself was missing more than its fair share of tiles and the chimney canted to the left, surrounded by a scattering of broken bricks. Around the structure wove a wooden verandah, again showing signs of age, with rotting timbers punctuating the once strong walkway. The grass around the house was churned in places, and there were tracks caused by vehicles driving in and out of the clearing. Crows cawed in the treetops high above them, their sudden flight making Crane jump.

"Wow," said Anderson.

"Holy fuck," said Crane, being of an altogether coarser breed of men. "Do you think it's locked up?"

"I shouldn't think there's any need," said Anderson pointing to the many broken panes of glass in the windows. "Come on, let's try the door first though."

The timbers creaked as they mounted the steps of the verandah, matching the creak of their leather shoes, with Crane's bootee-covered stick providing an uneven, muffled beat as an accompaniment. Anderson had insisted they suit up before going in, as should it be a crime scene, he once again didn't want any margin for error. Anderson pushed open the unlocked door which made the old rusted hinges creak.

"Straight out of a Hammer Horror movie," said Anderson showing his age, as he surveyed the large open room before them. It appeared that smaller rooms had had their dividing walls taken down, from the marks on the ceilings and corresponding ones on the floor, opening up the space to encompass the whole footfall of the house. Everywhere Crane looked there was evidence of Satanic rituals. The walls were adorned with signs and symbols. Black robes were incongruously hung on hooks around the walls, reminiscent of a classroom cloakroom, and in the middle of the room was a large structure, covered in black material, which was clearly an altar. A clutch of black candles adorned the top, with a solitary white one in their midst.

"The movies used props to create something like this," said Crane. "But these aren't props, they're for real." Crane spied a set of stairs. "Seems there's a basement," he said and he pointed to a set of stairs descending into inky blackness.

Moving over to take a closer look, Anderson said, "They're very steep and some of the treads are rotten. Stay here, it's safer."

"But,"

"But nothing, Crane. I don't want you breaking your bloody neck as well as your hip. You'll be no good to me then, will you?"

As Anderson inched his way down the stairs, the light of his torch bouncing with every step, Crane had to take deep breaths to contain his frustration. He wanted nothing more than to go down and see for himself.

As Anderson reached the bottom, Crane shouted, "Anything?"

"Just a minute, man."

Anderson's torch moved out of Crane's sight, leaving a thick blackness behind that Crane's eyes couldn't penetrate. Not the most patient of men, Crane blurted, "Derek?" and was rewarded with the rustling of Anderson's suit as he walked back to the stairs.

"Nothing. There's no one here, just an empty cell where the girls must have been kept."

"Thank God there wasn't another one down there," said Crane as Anderson emerged from the basement.

"Let's get out of here and call for forensics before we do any more damage to the crime scene."

As Crane peeled off his suit by the car, Anderson spoke to the team at Bullock's house, requesting additional personnel come to the house in the woods.

"We're a bit busy here, DI Anderson," the supervisor of the forensics team said. "I can't spare anyone at the moment." Crane heard through the speaker on the mobile.

"Why?" Anderson sounded none too pleased.

"Because we've found a body buried in the garden. We think it's his wife. So now we've to process out here as well as indoors."

"Well someone will have to come and secure the scene while we wait for you. I'll get some uniforms up here. Just be as quick as you can will you?" and Anderson snapped shut the phone.

Sixty Eight

Once released from protecting the old house, by two uniformed officers, Crane and Anderson returned to the police station to review the forensic evidence that had been gathered so far, to see what tied the cases to DS Bullock.

Crane, who had calmed down somewhat, looked up from his reading of the reports. "What do you think they did out at that old house?"

"Christ knows. In fact I don't think I want to know," said Anderson.

"Do you think it really is the scene of a full blown Satanic cult, or sect, or grotto, whatever you want to call it?"

"Well, it all looked quite genuine."

"Oh, so you're a specialist on the occult are you now?" Crane laughed.

"You know what I mean. The signs, symbols and those Rules of the Earth that you found on the internet, were all painted on the walls. There were gowns and hoods for them to wear. Black candles on the altar, so I guess so."

"I wonder what they did?"

"Well I don't," snapped Anderson. "Can we get on with reading about what we do know, instead of speculating about what we don't?"

"Sure, sorry," Crane bent his head once more to the report, but then said, "I think we need a list."

"What? For Christ's sake, Crane, leave me alone."

"Alright," Crane said and stood and went over to the whiteboard, where he cleaned a portion of it and began to write.

He hadn't got very far when Anderson said, "Okay you win. What's that all about?"

Trying very hard not to grin, Crane revealed his bullet points. "These are things we need to interview Bullock about. I just needed to get it all straight in my head as there are so many possible charges."

"Go on then, let's go through them."

Grabbing his stick Crane pointed to the first line. "In no particular order, we need to talk to Bullock about:

1. *Enid Bullock*. She's been found dead, buried in the garden. His garden. A fork and spade were in clear view on the patio, covered in earth and his finger prints. The working theory at the moment is that she was strangled as upon initial examination Major Martin can find no other injuries, only bruising around her neck. It seems she's been dead for a few days. The Major will know more at the autopsy.

2. *Mr and Mrs Underwood*. They were found dead in their bed when their house was burned down. Petrol was the accelerant and the post mortem revealed they were alive when the fire started. DS Bullock was seen purchasing petrol the night of the fire at the local petrol station. We expect a forensic examination of his car will provide us with evidence of petrol inside it and possibly ash from the blaze. We may even find hairs on his suit

from the old people.

3. *The farmhouse.* There is evidence of Satanic rituals taking place there and evidence of the girls being held captive in the basement. We'll know more when the forensics come in, but I bet Bullock's, Clay's and the girls' fingerprints will be found there.

4. *Clay.* We think he was the one who lured the girls to his ice-cream van, drugged them and then took them to the farmhouse. This is supported by Bethany's evidence. Bullock is in the frame for murdering him by hitting him with that plank of wood, by virtue of his ginger hair left on the body.

5. *Bethany.* She managed to escape from the farmhouse and her body has given us evidence that they used her and her blood for their rituals. She also helped with the ice cream van ruse and identified Clay as her abductor. Bullock recently tried to kill her, no doubt in an attempt to shut her up, as she clearly could identify him as being one of the people at the farmhouse.

6. *Dawn.* Most likely her murder was an accidental overdose. But we can charge him with abduction, attempted murder of Bethany and abduction and murder of Dawn. Even if he didn't do it himself, he is still culpable."

As he finished, Crane sat down with a thump on the nearest chair, his stick between his legs and his hands and forehead resting on the top of it, sick to his stomach at the crimes perpetrated by, and the evidence against, Bullock. Lifting his head and looking at his friend he said, "And all this done by a man who was a police officer. Sworn to tell the truth and to uphold the law. What on earth possessed him?"

"The devil."

Sixty Nine

Left alone, DS Bullock had had to wait to be interviewed again and also to wait until his solicitor or Federation representative arrived. As the interminable day dragged on and on, with no distractions, flashes of the past began to flicker in his head like lightening. Appearing and then disappearing just as swiftly. Bursting brightly before burning out. He heard Enid choke, he felt his hands around her neck, he smelled smoke and flames and burning, he saw the flickering of candles on the altar, he watched his fellow supplicants engaged in their rituals, heard the bell ring nine times, saw the pubescent girl on the altar, once again tasted her blood on his lips.

It wasn't his fault. None of it. He'd bothered no one. He'd just wanted to be able to get on with his worship, with his way of life, in peace. But oh no, they wouldn't leave him alone. None of them. It was entirely their fault. They'd pushed him to his limits. Enid, her parents, stupid Clay. Why hadn't they all just left him alone?

The flame of anger grew inside him, fanned by the bloody idiot of a solicitor who, when he'd eventually arrived, was of no use at all. Apparently he had no experience of police interviews, as he mostly dealt with house purchases. Bullock knew more about criminal prosecutions than he did.

Apparently he was sent as he was the only one in the office who was free to come. It seems no one wanted to get involved with the prosecution of a police officer. He may have well have asked for a Duty Solicitor for all the use Rainworth was going to be. And the Police Federation said the local rep was off sick, they promised to get someone to travel to Aldershot, but it wouldn't be until the next day at the earliest.

And then they came for him; bloody Crane and Anderson, who walked into the room as if they owned the place.

In an attempt to calm himself down he began to recite the Rules of the Earth in his head.

"Thank you both for your patience," said Anderson to Bullock his solicitor. "Sorry for the wait."

Sorry? Sorry? Is that all Anderson had to say? Bullock was losing the fragile calmness that reciting his Rules had given him.

"Have you had time to confer with you client, Mr Rainworth?"

"Yes, um, sort of DI Anderson."

"What does sort of mean?"

"Well he won't talk to me."

Bullock wondered if Anderson and Rainworth had forgotten that he was in the room. They seemed determined to talk over him. To ignore him as much as possible.

"Ah, I can see your difficulty, but that's not actually our problem is it? So shall we proceed?" Turning at last to Bullock, Anderson addressed him directly and said, "It seems you've a fair few troubles, DS Bullock. Want to tell us about them?"

"Do not tell your troubles to others unless you are sure they want to hear them."

Anderson looked confused. "I beg your pardon?"

"Do not tell your troubles to others unless you are sure they want to hear them." Bullock repeated. "And I'm pretty sure you don't genuinely want to hear them. You don't give a toss about me and my problems and you never have. You've hated me from the first day I got here."

Ignoring what he'd just said, Anderson then asked him, "What about Enid? Why did you kill her?"

"Do not take that which does not belong to you, unless it is a burden to the other person and they cry out to be relieved."

"What the hell does that mean?" Crane burst out.

Anderson said, "I'm not sure if your client is fit to be questioned, Mr Rainworth, perhaps we should suspend the interview and call a doctor."

Rainworth said, "Um, I don't know, DI Anderson. I've not had much experience of this type of thing."

It seemed that everyone in the room was stupid, apart from himself thought Bullock, so with a shake of his head at their ignorance, he had to explain it to them.

"Enid was bowed under the weight of her troubles with her parents. They had taken over her life. She had no life left of her own at all, constantly carrying the burden of her elderly parents. So I decided to relieve her of the burden of living."

"Are you saying you killed Enid, DS Bullock?"

Bullock didn't reply.

"What about her parents? The Underwoods? Did you kill them as well?"

Bullock looked down at the table. *"If someone bothers you, ask them to stop."*

But it seemed Anderson wouldn't stop.

"How about Clay? What did he do wrong? Did he kill

those girls?"

"*Do not harm little children.*"

Anderson turned to Crane. "What did you just say?"

"It's in the Satanic Rules. Do not harm little children, isn't it Bullock? That's why you killed Clay because of what he'd done to the girls."

"Stop, just stop asking me these stupid questions, I've done nothing wrong," Bullock said. Sweat was breaking out all over his face now and he was wringing his hands in agitation.

"Yes you have, you tried to kill Bethany only this morning," said Anderson.

"Stop, stop, stop."

"And you've killed Dawn, Clay, your wife and her parents."

Pushed to the limit Bullock banged his fists down on the table and roared, "*If someone bothers you, ask them to stop. If they do not stop, destroy them!*"

And without any warning he stood and tipped up the table with the strength of a man possessed.

Anderson managed to move out of the way by falling sideways out of his chair, but Crane, slowed by his injuries, was pinned underneath it. Looking around, Bullock saw Crane trying and failing to lift the table off him and Rainworth cowering in the corner and crying.

Flinging himself at Anderson, he grabbed the policeman by the throat, shouting, "*If they do not stop destroy them!*" repeatedly banging Anderson's head against the floor and squeezing his neck, squeezing like he'd done with Enid, squeezing the life out of Anderson so he couldn't bother him anymore.

Seventy

The next thing that Anderson knew was that he was somewhere quiet and white. For a moment he wondered if he was in Heaven, but then occasional beeping disturbed the peace and every now and then he felt the contraction of a blood pressure cuff on his arm. The sight of Crane sat by his bed clinched it. He couldn't be in Heaven, for surely Crane wouldn't be there as well. He didn't believe God would be that cruel. Anderson laughed at his own wit but only a gurgling sound came out that made Crane snap up his head from his examination of his hands. Or had he been praying? Surely not.

"Anderson, thank God!"

Maybe Crane had been praying after all. He looked strained, but not like he usually did from the pain, this was much more primeval. There were was fear mixed in there as well. Had his friend thought he was going to die? Anderson tried to speak, but again only a strange croak came out.

"Don't speak, your larynx and throat are injured. Hang on I've got to get the Doctor. He wanted to know when you were awake."

Anderson had loads of questions running through his head on a loop, but had to subject himself to an examination by the doctor. Once he'd been prodded and poked and left alone, Crane said, "So, as the Doc has just said, you won't be able to speak for a few days, thank the Lord for small mercies," and grinned.

Anderson scowled at his friend.

"Oh, right, sorry, but we were more concerned about the head injury. You've got concussion and have been unconscious for 24 hours, but it seems you're on the mend. Look, I've got you a pencil and paper so you can write instead of speak."

Pushing himself upwards onto his pillows, Anderson grabbed the writing implements from Crane and wrote - Bullock?

"Still in custody. A bit battered and bruise from where officers pulled him off you, but he'll live."

- You?

"Fine, no damage done. I just couldn't get up. The table pinned my good leg down and I just didn't have the strength in my other one to help me get up off the floor."

- Solicitor?

Crane laughed, "Shocked but okay. I don't think he'll walk back into a police station any time soon though."

- Home?

Your wife and kids have been here. They've only just left so the Doc is going to ring them and let them know you're awake."

Anderson was finding this one sided conversation very frustrating and wrote - Go Home?

"Not a chance. You need to stay here another few days, until the Doc says you're okay to leave."

Bugger that, Anderson thought and fumbled with the

bed covers, flinging them back and swinging his legs out of the bed. But the action made his head swim, he started sweating and his hands trembled.

"Not so fast, Derek," Crane said, pushing Anderson back onto the bed. "If you don't behave I'll get the Doc to knock you out."

Anderson sank back on the pillows, for the moment defeated. But he'd try to get out of bed again as soon as the room stopped spinning and his stomach stopped feeling like he was riding a roller coaster.

Seventy One

The first place Anderson wanted to go to when he got out of the hospital was not home, but the police station. Something Crane wasn't surprised by. When the police car transporting them from the hospital pulled up in the car park, Anderson shook off Crane's helping hand and stormed into the custody suite.

- Show me Bullock, he wrote and showed the note to the Desk Sergeant.

They all looked at the monitor, which showed a large picture feed from Bullock's cell.

He was lying on the plastic covered thin mattress. The man's ginger hair was dishevelled, he was unwashed and unshaven, and his clothes crumpled and scruffy looking. His dress shirt was grimy and creased, the sleeves rolled up to his elbow. His trousers appeared to be falling down without his belt and his feet were clad in socks, his shoes being outside his cell placed next to his door.

As if sensing they were watching, Bullock sat up and stared at the CCTV camera located high up on the wall of his cell.

His gaze didn't waver and in the end it was Anderson who nodded to his fellow officers and turned away from the monitor.

- Charges? wrote Anderson in the small notebook he carried in the pocket of his beige raincoat.

"Attempted murder of one DI Anderson," said Crane.

- Not good enough.

"I know that, Derek, but Superintendent Grimes said it was the one we could slap on him straight away, whilst we waited for conclusive evidence on the other charges. It was a good job that he did attack you, by the way, otherwise we only had an initial 24 hours to put a case together complete with forensic evidence."

- Magistrate!

"We're well aware we could have got an additional 48 hours from a Magistrate, thank you very much, but we were all rather more concerned about you. Don't forget you were lying in a hospital bed, unconscious with swelling on the brain."

Anderson looked frustrated, but in the end wrote

- Okay.

Followed by a rather begrudging,

- Sorry.

But once they got to Anderson's office, it was clear Anderson wasn't going to leave the subject of Bullock alone.

Sitting in his chair behind his still cluttered desk, Anderson wrote

- Throw the book at him!

"Bloody hell, Derek, of course Grimes will," Crane sat in front of Anderson's desk, looking at his friend's pale face and the angry black and yellow bruises that could be seen, forming a necklace of thumb and finger prints around his throat.

- Need justice for girls.

"Don't we all, Derek. Bullock needs to go to prison for murder and kidnap for the rest of his life. But we have to wait for the evidence. You know it takes a long time for all the tests to be completed."

Crane was desperately trying to rein in his temper. He had to understand that his friend was injured and angry. That thought made Crane smile, for he knew more than enough about how it felt to be injured and being frustrated and angry about it.

"It's been a tense time for all of us, the whole team, from Grimes all the way down to DC Douglas."

Anderson nodded his understanding.

"From the results of all the tests we already have," Crane continued, "we have built a case against Bullock for most of the murders and attempted murders."

Anderson frowned

- Most of?

Shit. It seemed Anderson had picked up on Crane's frustration about one of the charges. He must practice his blank look; it seemed he was a little rusty still.

"It's the old people, the Underwoods."

- What about them?

"Well, the fire was definitely started with petrol, according to the fire brigade, but we haven't any witnesses to say it was Bullock, nor fingerprint or other evidence. Anyway if his prints were found there, he would naturally say that it was from previous visits. After all they were his parents-in-law."

- There must be more!

"I know, Derek. But I just don't know what it is."

- Find something. I'm going home.

"Yes, boss," said Crane.

Seventy Two

Once left alone, Crane asked DC Douglas to bring all the evidence gathered from DS Bullock's house. Commandeering a table in the incident room, Crane and Douglas spread all the packets and tubes across the table.

"What are we looking for, sir?" asked Douglas.

"Something to tie Bullock to the fire at the Underwood's house."

"Like what?"

"I've no bloody idea."

"Ah, a needle in a haystack job."

Did Douglas actually look happy about such a search? Crane was sure he'd just seen the man's eyes flash with interest.

Crane grumbled, "Something like that, but in this case we don't even know what the bloody needle looks like."

"Oh. Right."

Douglas' reply was rather more subdued, which was about right, as Crane felt they had an uphill struggle on this one.

But he wouldn't let Anderson down. He'd show him and the rest of the police team that he was good at his job. As good as them, if not better.

A grumbling hip and gammy leg wasn't going to stop him doing what he was good at. He had been a bloody good army investigator and he was determined that he would be equally as good a police investigator.

That thought made Crane pause in his perusal of the evidence. Had he just been positive and determined? He reckoned he had and the thought straightened his spine and squared his shoulders.

He looked at the stick in his left hand. Could he? Should he? He stood dithering.

"You alright, boss?" Douglas broke though Crane's reverie.

"Couldn't be better," Crane replied and walked into Anderson's office.

He took off his suit jacket and put it around the back of a chair, rolled up his shirt sleeves and went back to join Douglas. Leaving his stick behind.

It was a long job. Each piece of evidence had been logged and Crane and Douglas had to cross reference it with the murder book to see what theory it substantiated. Nearly an hour had gone by before Crane came across a small paper ticket.

"Any idea what this is, Douglas?"

Douglas joined Crane and took the packet from him.

"No, sorry. Don't remember seeing that before."

Crane took it back and looked at it more closely. He checked with the files but there was no notation that the ticket had been attributed to any charge. Or that there had been any follow-up on it.

Limping into the office, Crane got a magnifying glass out of Anderson's desk, for once ignoring the chocolate treats in there.

Peering through the glass he read the small logo; *Bright's.*

Underneath this word was a number. One edge of the ticket was jagged, as though it had been torn out of a book.

Bright's. Crane considered the name. He considered where Bullock lived - Farnborough. Ignoring his laptop, Crane pulled a telephone directory off the shelf behind Anderson's desk and thumbed through it.

"You got something, boss?"

Crane hadn't heard Douglas come up behind him and jumped at the young man's voice.

"You know I think I have," said Crane and pointed to the open page.

"Dry Cleaners," Douglas read out loud.

"Exactly," said Crane. "More specifically Bright's Dry Cleaners in Farnborough. Right, get someone to put away that lot," he pointed at the evidence spread around the table, "and then you can drive me to Farnborough."

***

The dry cleaners looked less bright and more grey as the exterior of the shop looked in need of a facelift.

The paint was peeling off the sign and the entrance door. There was a metal roller security screen that wasn't pushed all the way back and multi-coloured graffiti could be seen adorning the bottom of it. The windows were grubby and in need of a wash and the window frames had hardly any paint left on them.

But once inside, there was a transformation.

The shop was spotlessly clean and tiled from floor to ceiling. The room smelled of bleach mingling with dry cleaning fluid and the temperature inside was significantly warmer than outside.

Crane introduced himself and Douglas and then

showed the owner of the business, Mrs Bright, the ticket which was still in the evidence bag.

"Is this one of your tickets?" he asked.

"Oh yes, that's one of ours."

"Could you tell me who the customer was?"

"Should be able to," she said and pulled a paperback book from under the counter.

She quickly found the correct ticket number and said, "We always take a name and phone number and this one is in the name of Bullock. Here," she turned the book around and pushed it towards Crane.

He looked at it, with Douglas peering from his position beside Crane.

"Do you know the customer in question?"

"Oh yes, Mr Bullock is a regular customer. A policeman of some sort I think. Always very nice and so is his wife. They regularly bring in Mr Bullock's suits."

"Is that what this ticket is for? A suit?"

"I'll go and get it for you," she said.

After a brief pause she returned, holding a suit by the coat hanger it was placed on. The suit was encased in a plastic wrapper with a note attached to it with a safety pin.

"What's that," asked Douglas, pointing to the note.

She expertly swung the suit onto the table and laid it out flat.

Mrs Bright read the note.

"Ah, yes, I remember now," she said. "When Mr Bullock brought the suit in he arrived just after 9 am. I'd just opened up. The suit smelled terribly of petrol and smoke. You know that bonfire type of smell?"

Crane nodded.

"It was so strong I asked him what had happened. I needed to know, you see, because the type of stain depends on how we clean it."

"And what did he say?"

Crane couldn't believe what was happening. He was leaning in slightly towards Mrs Bright and her counter, his fingers mentally crossed. Could this be what they had been waiting for?

"He said he'd been involved in a house fire. It had been started with petrol and he'd tried to rescue the occupants."

"And who were the occupants, did he say?"

"Oh, yes, he told me all about them. They were his parents in law, Mr and Mrs Underwood, but they hadn't made it unfortunately."

Crane was sure that by now his eyes were out on stalks.

"I offered my condolences, but there was something a bit strange about his reaction."

"Which was?" Douglas croaked.

"It was as if he was glad they were dead, not sad. He said not to worry, that when it's your time, it's your time. Then he gave me a big smile and left."

Crane could have kissed her. Now he had something to take to Anderson – a clear link between the fire and the petrol and Bullock.

Seventy Three

As Anderson's voice was still very much hit and miss, it fell to Crane to give Diane Chambers an interview, which was the quid pro quo arranged with her for the splash in the Aldershot News on the missing girl. It was essentially a summary of the case. Diane sat there, with her mobile and note book, but Crane noticed she no longer wore her trademark jeans, tee-shirt and checked shirt over it. Instead she was wearing a trouser suit. The white tee-shirt was still very much in evidence though, underneath her smarter outer wear. Maybe Diane was getting serious about her career in her old age, thought Crane. But he decided to keep those observations to himself. The last thing he needed was to inadvertently rub her up the wrong way. The subsequent fall-out would be too costly.

When they'd finished, or Crane hoped they had, she relaxed and leaned back in her chair. "So you're working for the police now then, Crane? That's a news story in itself you know, Sgt Major."

"You don't need to use my title, Diane. I'm not in the army anymore."

"Clearly, but I'm sure my readers want to know why you're not and in what capacity you are working for the police."

Crane felt like scowling, but instead tried very hard to put on a happy face, as though the questions didn't bother him. "Don't you dare, Diane, don't you dare go there," he said in what he hoped was a jokey voice, but rather thought it wasn't.

Chambers was quick to pick up on it. "Oh, are you sure? Maybe I won't mention it if there's anything else I could put it in its place? Another story related to this one maybe? One that would push a piece about you off the page?"

Crane hated Diane's ability to outmanoeuvre people and manipulate conversations and change answers to give her the one she wanted in the first place. Crane pretended to think, although he'd had a suspicion before they met that it would come to this.

"How about this instead? You could praise Blake and Mimi from Totlands Total Tattoo. Their two their calls to us about sulphur tattoos that customers had requested, really helped the enquiry. And I'm sure they'd appreciate the publicity."

Actually Crane privately thought that Blake wouldn't want to be publically associated with the police, but hey if there was going to be a fall guy, it certainly wasn't going to be him.

Seventy Four

A celebration of sorts was taking place at Crane's house. He and Tina had invited Derek and his wife Jean to dinner and much to his relief there were no major crimes to be investigated that night, to ruin the celebratory meal.

Anderson pushed his plate away and said, "Tina, that was wonderful. I'm sure I've consumed too many calories, but what the heck."

Crane was pleased to hear his friend's voice had become stronger, only cracking occasionally and when it did Anderson normally disguised it with a cough, although he wasn't really fooling anyone.

Jean reached for the wine bottle. "Refill anyone?" to which they all nodded. No one had to drive that night as Derek and Jean were to go home in a taxi at the end of the evening.

"How are you feeling now, Derek?" Tina asked.

"Much better thanks, a bit frustrated with the old voice, but the doctors say it'll come back stronger than ever, but I've not to speak much in the meantime."

"Thank goodness," spoke up Jean. "The house is much quieter without Derek shouting at the kids."

"How can you say that, woman," Derek said and they all laughed at his mock outrage. "Anyway there's something else to celebrate, other than the closing of the case."

"There is?" asked Crane.

"Jean you're not?" said Tina.

Jean shook her head. "No, this one is nothing to do with me."

"Come on then, Derek," said Tina. "Don't keep us in suspense."

"You're retiring," guessed Crane.

"No chance, you'll not get rid of me that easily. No, it's to do with you, Crane."

Crane's heart sank. It was probably some sort of commendation for helping with the case. But that was not what he wanted at all.

"You were such a help with the case and got on so well with everyone, especially DC Douglas, that Grimes and I had a few words."

"Which were?" said Tina.

Derek reached into his inside pocket. "This is for you, Crane."

Crane took the long white envelope with his name typed on it, but didn't open it. Just stared at it.

"Oh for God's sake, Derek, stop it," said Jean bumping his arm. "Just tell us will you?"

Derek grinned. "We've created a new post. Criminal Consultant to the Major Crimes team, which consists of myself, DC Douglas and Holly. And the first incumbent of the post is Sgt Major Crane (Retired)."

Meet the Author

I do hope you've enjoyed Rules of the Earth If so, perhaps you would be kind enough to post a review on Amazon. Reviews really do make all the difference to authors and it is great to get feedback from you, the reader.

If this is the first of my novels you've read, you may be interested in the other Sgt Major Crane books, following Tom Crane and DI Anderson as they take on the worst crimes committed in and around Aldershot Garrison. At the time of writing there are eight Sgt Major Crane crime thrillers. In order, they are: Steps to Heaven, 40 Days 40 Nights, Honour Bound, Cordon of Lies, Regenerate, Hijack, Glass Cutter and Solid Proof.

Past Judgment is the first in a new series. It is a spin-off from the Sgt Major Crane novels and features Emma Harrison from Hijack and Sgt Billy Williams of the Special Investigations Branch of the Royal Military Police. The second book, Mortal Judgment and the third, Joint Judgement have just been released. Look out for more adventures from Billy and Emma in the Judgment series in the near future.

All my books are available on Amazon.

You can keep in touch through my website http://www.wendycartmell.webs.com. I'm also on Twitter @wendycartmell.

Printed in Great Britain
by Amazon